Fox running on the far side of Lake Wasatch, breakfast pizza taste still in her mouth. She has found a faint path that winds between a break line of poplars and the Uinta foothills. In her easy, swinging stride she moves through a tunnel of leaves. Her eyes scan the ground, her bare feet chuffchuffchuffchuff the dust. She rounds a bend of the widening trail. Suddenly she goes knee-deep in goldenrod. She stops to roll in these chaffy weeds. Yellow-headed blackbirds croak from the tules. Lapping water draws Fox to the lake's edge, where she stops for a sip and prints in the mud. She leaves her mark for Sudden to find:

FOX RUNNING≫→

FOX RUNNING

A NOVEL BY

R.R. Knudson

Drawings by Ilse Koehn

 AVON
PUBLISHERS OF BARD, CAMELOT, DISCUS, EQUINOX AND FL

AVON BOOKS
A division of
The Hearst Corporation
959 Eighth Avenue
New York, New York 10019

Published by arrangement with Harper & Row, Publishers.
Library of Congress Catalog Card Number: 75-6294
ISBN: 0-380-00930-7

First Avon Printing, February, 1977

AVON TRADEMARK REG. U.S. PAT. OFF. AND IN
OTHER COUNTRIES, MARCA REGISTRADA,
HECHO EN U.S.A.

Printed in the U.S.A.

For Rachel MacKenzie, who runs with her pen

1

Bang.

The passing truck backfired at a tall shadow running down the middle of Highway 40. That shadow swayed, nearly fell forward, then straightened and ran again. Ran fast.

Ran fifty yards ahead of the onrushing Thunderbird. Ran along the yellow center line while the car's harsh headlights picked shadowy feet out of the night. Inside the Thunderbird, Kathy "Sudden" Hart stared at the runner, then turned to the driver and said, "No shoes, Coach. Those feet must be roasting."

Tar glistened under the bare toes that turned quickly right, sprinting for the shoulder of Highway 40. Long legs kept running there. Fast.

"No running shoes but what a stride! Check that knee action. Wow!" Sudden gave a whoop of joy.

Coach Guy Calvin wasn't impressed. "Some drunk loose on the road," he grouched. He slowed the car. He dimmed the lights, sending a low beam after the runner, who now sped thirty, twenty-five, twenty, only fifteen feet ahead. Its big feet plowed the sand. Its legs surged like pistons. Its balled-up hands, bare elbows swung in rapid cadence. A single braid of black hair flapped a running rhythm. "Stride's too even for a drunk," said Calvin in a minute. "Long, long stride at that. Say—beautiful."

"That's a . . ." Sudden started.

"Smooth. Powerful. Splendid runner!"

"Girl. That's a girl," Sudden announced.

Coach Calvin whistled. "She's mighty fast." He blinked in appreciation. "She's very strong. Look at that muscle structure."

Sudden held her breath, enjoying the sight: a tall girl running swiftly, gracefully in the car's headlights. "She can really step it."

Calvin whistled again. "Considering the miserable track conditions, she's unbelievable. She must be pushing through a foot of sand and gravel."

"Tough soles she wears. That sand must be full of briars —scorpions—jagged rocks." Sudden moved her foot, pretending to jam on the brakes. "Coach, stop the car. Let's watch her for a while."

Calvin pulled his Thunderbird alongside the running girl and stopped. She didn't. She sped to the car's hood, wheeled, faced the driver for an instant, turned again, and raced beyond the headlights.

"Was only an Indian," came a dozy voice from the backseat. Champion Davis' voice.

"She has a quick start, like Sudden's," said the Coach. "Like Sudden's in the good old days. Wake up and look again, Champion. The girl's running on asphalt, faster than ever." Coach Calvin flicked high beam and low gear, said, "Look at her fly," to his own two runners, and set off in admiring pursuit.

Sudden whispered to a sleepy Champ, "She's a natural."

"She's all yours. I'm falling back to sleep." Champ stretched on the leather upholstery. He patted his ginger hair. He smoothed his suit jacket and vest. "Yours."

Sudden said, "She has great balance. She makes you want to know those muscles. But her start didn't seem practiced. More like fright. And did you see her eyes in the headlights? Looked scared."

An oncoming car broke the spell. Coach slowed his Thunderbird, steered carefully, watching the speeding heels to his right. "She's sprinting flat out. Where did she get that big kick?" he asked himself.

"I'm more wondering what she's doing around here. Who she's running from—and—and what her feet are paved with. She scuffs cactus without a wince. My Adidas shoes should be so thick."

Caught now in four shafts of light, the Indian girl veered from tar to sand to sagebrush, jumping low clumps with no breaks in stride. "Watch her vault that juniper, Sudden." Calvin poked his front-seat companion and pointed at the figure hurdling one bush, then another. He whistled louder. "How can she get such spring out of this soil?"

Sudden hung on each step. Bursts of earth flew back

8

from the Indian girl's heels as she took off, landed, took off, landed, took off again over scraggly junipers. A full yellow moon lit her path—parallel to Route 40 and north of it maybe five yards. She ran west with the cruising Thunderbird.

Another jump, this one over chaparral, and Calvin nearly leaped out of his plush bucket seat. "Wake up, Champ. She's running *your* event. The hurdles. And better than you, my boy. Her rhythm's smoother, even though she's on this irregular course. Champ—Sudden— what she could do on our track team!"

Champ didn't budge. He seemed asleep. Sudden whispered, "Who let her out of the blocks? Who fired the starter's gun?" Aloud she said, "That girl can do it all," and moved to lower the window for a better view. Calvin quickly pressed a row of buttons on his side. All windows glided down. A mileage counter whirled back to zero. The glove box dropped open. "Hand me my stopwatch, Sudden, and my camera—there, with the wide lens. Call the girl over here. I want to get some shots of her leg action while I time her in this stretch." He began wiggling a strobe light into place, mumbling, "A desert runner. Alone. In the dark, and yet a flash."

Sudden poked her head out the window and gave out with a robust, "Hey," then broke off, wondering what to yell next. What name? Who? "Hey, Runner. Wait up." Sudden waved and hit the side of the Thunderbird. Bam. Bam.

"She can't hear. Too far ahead of us," Calvin yelled over the yowling horn.

Champ sat up in the backseat, arranging his cuff links. "Where are we? . . . Why the blitz? . . . What?" He squinted out the back window. "Oh, that Indian, running again."

"Running *still*. She's never rested."

Champ rubbed his eyes. "Hoo, she's swift. Nothing wrong with that. What's her time for this lap?"

"Time for you to hurdle out and catch her," Calvin said, stopping the car and tugging his door lock. "I've got to take pictures or no one will believe me."

Sudden climbed out. "Not to worry, you guys. Sit there. She's on her way. See, she's coming directly at us."

But she wasn't. She saw the big car with left door swinging and the other door standing open. She saw a

9

short shape waiting near the hood, saw two larger shapes lurking inside, saw a pair of flashing red taillights—and she bolted right, over a ragged row of mesquite and off into the desert. Sudden watched the glossy braid shorten, wide shoulders narrow, long legs become stumps as the Indian girl ran, ran out of vision.

Coach shouted, "Go get her, Champion."

"Me? A world-class track man chase her?"

"She'll run out of range."

Coach clicked his camera.

"So let her. So what?" Champ sounded crosser and crosser.

"We could use her on the team." Calvin reset his stopwatch. He reached for a zoom lens. "What's the matter, Champ? Afraid you can't outrun her?"

Champ didn't bother to answer.

Sudden, darting off the shoulder and into the night, called, "Not to worry. I'll catch her."

2

Two figures now speeding across the desert: the frontrunner taller, stronger, faster, and more mysterious than before. Or so it seemed to Sudden, who ran flat out with shorter, jerkier strides that were, however, no less swift. Sudden kept the pace. She kept dead straight except when thorns caught the wide cuffs of her slacks, pulling her slightly off course. She shucked off cactus, stayed balanced, and ran on. Her bulky cardigan heated her up. Her shirt collar pinched her straining neck muscles. Her sockless feet chafed in her Adidas Olympias, which filled with sand as she ran.

Blazing a moonlit trail, bare feet whispered to the ground as they hopped prairie-dog holes, dodged piñons, turned ninety degrees to avoid a steep incline. The Indian ran silently. Sudden couldn't even hear her breathing. After all those yards, meters, miles probably—no

10

gasping from that girl. Her lungs must be huge, thought Sudden, who began to breathe heavily. "I'm out of shape," she said to herself. But panting, grunting, Sudden gained ground.

"Wait up, will you?" she called. Her voice flew forward. She followed, gaining more.

The surefooted leader ran mute. Her hair had come loose and streamed behind, a thick black tail. Her T-shirt, wet with effort, clung to her. Her rawhide belt came undone, her raveling shorts hung lower on her narrow hips, exposing a wide patch of gleaming skin.

"You're losing your pants," Sudden called, not so loud. She was closer. No need.

No answer.

"Let down your shoulders. Shake both hands. Stay loose. You're tightening up."

Not a word.

"Don't let your head roll back. Shortens your stride," Sudden offered—good running advice.

Not a nod.

"You're losing form completely," Sudden whispered.

But still they ran through the moony night. Past sleeping quail and roadrunners. Over rabbit warrens. Alongside mescal plants. Across a gully and along the rim of a ravine. Four feet slurred through sand, struck firmer ground, then pebbles and sharp stones. Sudden kicked one of these to her right and listened for its drop.

Nothing. Nothing until a faint "Plink."

"Deep there," Sudden called. "Dangerous. Don't slip. Don't turn right!" Only those cautions from her furred tongue. No breath for more.

The suddenness of a runner so close behind caused a slight hitch in the Indian girl's stride. She swayed right, righter, right to the edge and almost over as her pursuer grabbed wildly for her fringy shorts. Sudden caught a wisp of cotton, stabbed again, caught a loop over the rear pocket, jerked herself closer, took a hammer hold of waist, and shoved the startled girl left, left—

Neither girl fell. Neither fell off the pace. Both missed only a few strides. They raced almost neck and neck now, Sudden's breath haunting the taller girl's ears. They broke downhill toward a stand of bushes, circled these, slung themselves uphill once more. Backtracking. Backtracking the longest time.

"Where now?" Sudden gasped at last. For reply only the coo-c-o-o of an owl. And a kit fox barked ahead.

From there a small wind funneled down the gulch, drying soaked foreheads and cheeks. The runners, refreshed, sped on. Back through beheaded paintbrush, trampled ragweed, stomped spiders, and vinegarroons. Back around anthills. Back over thistles, cockleburs. Tough soles. Some tough soles on that kid, Sudden kept thinking. And some beautiful stride after all those miles!

"You're magic," Sudden managed to whisper at last. "Magi . . ."

Then back toward red flashes, straight for the highway where Thunderbird waited with open doors. What's she up to, wondered Sudden. Why to the car? Or maybe she just can't see. Sweat salt's blinding in big doses. Her eyes must be full of it. Sudden slowed, swiped her own brow with her wrist, glanced ahead to see Champion's arm waving darkly from the front bumper: Champion's long arm.

"Can't you see Champ?" Sudden called. "Swerve off. That's Champ. He'll get you. Hang a right turn." Sudden stopped running altogether.

At that the car's horn set about a fearful yammering. Long blasts. Short beeps. Mixed. Menacing. The lone Indian sputtered, threw her fists in her eyes and ground them hard. She dipped her face down to her shirttail and rubbed. She looked up, around. She seemed to ask, "What now? Which way? Where should I run? Where is safe?" She bent double and groaned. Her hair-tail fell around her protectively, like a magic mantle. Then she stood and shuddered, unbent, walked, ran, sped again.

With Champ at her heels. Wide-awake Champ. Fresh Champ as if shot off the bumper from a dashboard button pushed by Calvin. Sudden watched him coursing, gaining ground. She saw him overtake and run his target to the sand. The girl lay panting. Gone to earth, Sudden thought, like an animal.

"I've got her," Champ called to his Coach.

12

3

"Well, well, my girl. You're quite a runner. Do you have a name to go with that speed?" Coach Guy Calvin began the questions that soon flew around his car.

Champ helped him. "Yeah, Smoke. What do they call you?"

"Who can she be?" Sudden wondered, half aloud. "Someone magic?"

The four of them rode through the August night. At the wheel, Coach Calvin set the Thunderbird's cruise control, loosened his seat belt, ran a hand through his spiky hair, and asked, "What's your name there, Runner?"

Silence.

"What happened to your shorts?"

More silence.

"Sudden, give our mystery guest one of your towels. Help her tie it like a sarong."

Sudden held the towel and said, "My suitcase—back in the trunk. I'll get her an extra uniform." She searched a pile of gear on the floor. "Here's my warm-up jacket— you can wrap—"

The Indian girl made no move to take the jacket.

"Or we could drive back to her running grounds and look for those lovely cut-off carpenter's pants she lost in the final two hundred twenty yards," Champ said.

Sudden looked hard at Champion. "Just be glad they fell off. Broke her stride. You might of never caught up."

"Oh yeah? I did better than you, Miss Has-Been. You ran a mile or more to catch her and didn't." Champ snorted. "I was about to grab the hammer loop when she fell." He held his wrists to a scrap of dashboard light. "How about these scratches she gave me before I could shove her into the backseat?"

Coach Calvin cut his eyes right at Champ and whistled.

"She's a vixen. Wash your hands when we stop for a snack in Flagstaff. I'll tape them." Then, looking in the rearview mirror, he asked the girl, "How long had you been running? Before we drove by? Before we stopped, I mean? How many hours? Days?"

Long silence.

Champ said, "She's not exactly gabby, is she, Coach? Let me try. I'll ferret something out."

He turned to watch the slim shadow hunched in the backseat. Watch it what? She's not moving a muscle, a hair, a pore. Just sits like red sandstone next to Sudden. From a shadowy runner to an animal to a wooden Indian —in minutes flat. Who could understand? Say, maybe she's dead from her run. Heart got her. "On with the light so's I can see, Coach. She might waggle her head or blink answers. Hey, Long Nails, you got a name?"

No wiggle.

"You realize you got mowed down by a famous hurdler? Me!"

No blink.

"You live out there?" Champ pointed, growing impatient.

Not a budge. Her black eyes were narrow slits. Her hands lay folded on the jacket tucked around her thighs. Champ looked for bloodstains—his—under her fingernails. "Long Nails," he muttered at length. He noted her wet hair tangled around her neck. He waited for her to push back the strands in her eyes or to toss her head or even to try an escape from her backseat lair. None of this happened.

"Two famous runners," said Coach after miles. "Sometimes, Champion, you seem to forget that Sudden's a gold medalist."

"And washed up at age nineteen. Anyway, I caught up with the Indian, not Sudden, Olympics or no Olympics. And I'll squeak answers out of her if she can understand English." He turned back to his prey. "She's just doing a little coyote, planning some sneaky move. How about that, Hiawatha?"

Quiet in the car.

"Bobcat got your tongue? Anyway, you run like one. *That* you can do."

Dead quiet in the car. The speedometer said seventy,

the fuel gauge half full. One blue square on the instrument panel clocked the hour to the second: 10:10.20. Another, the passing day: August 30. Calvin checked the second hand against his wristwatch, adjusted a climate-control lever, flipped on the map light, and read the green Interstate 40 line. "Not far now until a food break. I guess you're all hungry after running?" he asked.

Sudden admitted she was. Champ retied his bow tie and announced he hadn't even worked up a sweat, let alone an appetite, during his "desert romp." The other passenger said nothing.

"Do you want music with your questions?" asked Calvin, dialing the radio away from the news. "Or sports? A report of our track meet yesterday?" The rear-seat speakers throbbed.

Champ asked, "What for? I know *I won* my race, set a national record, tied another. Who needs a sports report? Unless they decide to interview *me* on the old airwaves. I'd give them the right answers: my super ability, my hard work . . ."

"Coaching," put in Sudden.

"My secret diet of health foods . . ."

"Coach Guy Calvin," Sudden tried again.

"Stamina, smarts—say, that's what I'll do! I'll give out with the answers. This girl can state the question, okay?"

Further silence, except the radio.

Champ said, "Here's an easy one for starters. *Wickiup. Wickiup.* Do I pronounce it just right?"

No question.

Champ said, "That answers 'Where do you live?' Nothing to it. My answers for your questions. You make them up. Take a shot at these. Scratching Girl. No Open Mouth."

Still no questions.

"Simple. What is your name, right? One of those names, right?"

Sudden answered, "Slim Cougar. Or Running Girl. Her name, I mean." She peered at Silent Girl, who had slumped down further as answers and questions filled the cool air. Sudden saw a dark profile, long lashes pointing straight ahead. She watched for a wink, a wince, as Champ kept giving answers like "Sharp Elbows."

"Navajo, Pima, Ute, Hualapai," Calvin broke in. "If we

15

knew her tribe we could figure out a lot more. Where she's from, for instance, and exactly what she might be doing around here." He paused. "We'll find out in Flagstaff. I'll call the state police." He clicked off the light, the radio, and said, "Soon."

Fewer cars lit up Interstate 40 as night deepened. The moon clouded over, stars failed to appear. The car's total darkness and untroubled, thumming engine soothed Champ. He murmured, "She runs pretty good, though. Maybe she's got a regular Anglo name—Mary Ann Elkshoulder or Judi Bearscomeout. . . ." He napped.

Sudden picked nettles from her shoelaces and thought about Silent Girl next to her. Perhaps she'd like a drink of leftover E.R.G. Should I offer? Guess not. Yet she must be thirsty after such a run. Woody mouthed, probably. Go on and try. No, she'll ignore you. She'll shoot you down with silence. Try anyway. No! Sudden went back and forth, afraid to offer, wanting to try, scared she'd be treated like Coach and Champion. She raked her fingers through her cuffs, combing out burrs. She listened for a sound of life from the corner.

Deep silence.

Sudden unlaced her shoes, took them off, emptied their sand out the window, and squished her feet in the rug. She massaged her insteps. She noticed blisters swelling on each heel. She fished around in the gear for cotton gauze, tape. She leaned forward, asked Coach quietly, "Where's the alcohol?"

A drowsy answer from Champ: "In my shaving kit, but don't let *her* at it. You've heard about firewater and Indians!"

Sudden blurted, "Oh, come off it, Pretty Boy. She hears you even if she doesn't speak. Quit insulting her." To herself Sudden whispered, "Patience, Hart. He's only eighteen and his head's puffed up from his big wins yesterday."

Champ faked yawns and asked, "How do you know she's not deaf? Besides, wouldn't matter if she could hear. She's thick-skinned. Hoo! Remember those bare feet on the thorny sands of New Mexico? She couldn't feel a prickle."

"How would you know, Thick Heart?" Then, in a whisper, "Patience, patience. He's just not used to being

16

ignored by the girls." Sudden shrugged off her damp sweater, folded it up, held out this pillow, saying, "Here, Miss—uh—for your head. Would you like a drink of our secret running formula? E.R.G.? It replaces sweat, sugar, everything you lost back there. Except your shorts." Sudden tried to laugh.

No "yes" from the girl. No "no." And no movement. Sudden sighed and dropped the sweater. She pressed her cheek against the cold window. She sat absolutely still, hard for her, watching nothing, hearing darkness, thinking zero—no, not even zero. Not thinking. Sudden tried to put herself in the Indian girl's place. She worked hard to blot out all feelings, thoughts. She tried to be a bump on a log. She longed to be a brick, brick red, a red Indian—unmoved, unmoving. She longed for—for about two minutes. Then she sat straight up and mumbled, "It can't be done. No one's that empty. It's impossible."

Calvin asked, "What are you muttering about, Sudden? Tell me as we eat a fast slice of pie. Special treat on me for Champ's wins and your stellar coaching. Champ, are you ready to drive?" He slowed the Thunderbird, looking for a restaurant. Neon blazed in Flagstaff.

And so did the backseat, with kaleidoscope colors from the signs. At that moment a slight move from the corner caught Sudden's attention. Sudden didn't turn to look. She didn't jump or anything. She listened and wondered what. Maybe unclasping hands? Unscrunching toes?

Sudden's ears held the sounds a long moment. At last she turned to face the watchful black eyes of the mysterious girl. Sudden watched back. "I'm Kathy, called Sudden," she said to the dark, closed face.

"Because she used to be so fast out of the starting blocks. Swift and sudden," Champion chimed in sleepily. "A winner. She could really run once."

"Still can," Calvin said. "You saw her back there in the desert. She flies the hundred any day or night when she wants to."

Sudden smiled and volunteered her whole name now. "I'm Kathy Hart—Hart."

"Gold-medal hundred. Winner in the Vienna Olympics." Calvin parked the car. "You felt her breathing down your neck. You felt her . . ."

Sudden kept trying. "I'm Hart. I only grabbed you

17

back there to keep both of us out of that bottomless ravine. I—I was enjoying our race. I wanted to find out who would win." She laughed a little. "I was rooting for you. Please—who are you?"

A low, clear voice beside her answered, "I am Fox Running."

4

At first light, the Uinta University campus seemed to Sudden a factory or prison spread at the base of Squaw Peak. She'd never considered from that distance the graying line of buildings that hugged the mountains: General Motors West or San Quentin East, she thought, the only head awake in the car to think.

And drive. She handled the Thunderbird with unusual ease, as though it were part of her body. She maneuvered the powerful car around milk vans and tractors like her own legs over obstacles in a steeplechase. She hurried the four of them north through the dawn, watching the rapid increase of recognizable buildings at Uinta.

"We're into the final lap—the gun lap," she whispered to her passengers. Champ and Coach Calvin snored. Fox Running slept—or pretended to.

The main library and a row of dormitories emerged from shadows of the Uinta Mountains. South of the counseling center the campus greenhouse caught first rays from the sun. Gold filled the hundred windows. Every pane of glass blinked a welcome to Sudden: "Come in."

Sun now over Utah. Gold in Sudden's eyes. She said, "Hand me my dark glasses."

No one handed. The rear-seaters slept. Fox Running, next to Sudden, reclined in the bucket seat like a papoose in her cradle. A real baby, this Fox. Tall, but not eighteen years old as she had whispered to them in Flagstaff. Extra tall, but not seventeen, Sudden felt sure. Maybe not even sixteen. Why had Coach believed Fox? He needs her for his team, that's why! He'd rob any cradle in America to win track meets! Well, almost any.

At Point-of-the-Mountain Sudden shifted to neutral and coasted the miles toward the UU greenhouse. She'd never really noticed it before. What's inside, she wondered. "Finish line on the horizon," she mentioned to anyone.

And just then Sudden's favorite sight rose from the foothills to greet her. The Cosmodome: world's largest college stadium and gym. Home of the Uinta University teams—the Indians. Utah's own Astrodome. Sudden broke into a good-morning smile as she zoomed for its glass dome. "See that round building up there, Fox. It's a runner's paradise," she said. Fox woke, looked here and there at cornfields and peach orchards.

"Right," she said softly.

Right. Fox's favorite word. Her one-word cover story, so Sudden had discovered when they all ate at the truck stop in Flagstaff.

Fox had sat there in the booth, handsome and sulky, refusing to be drawn into the conversation about track meets and medals. "Fox Running," she repeated. No rank, no age, no serial number. "Fox Running" answered every question. Less information than a captured soldier.

"Anyway, you look fine in Sudden's warm-up suit," Coach said after her fifth introduction. "What's your fastest hundred meters?" He watched Fox's sharp fingernails pick at number 10.5 on the jacket and added, "That's Sudden's racing number and best time—10.5 seconds in the Olympic hundred meters. Three years ago this month. A world record that no one's broken ever since. No one's likely to for years." He sipped his milk. "Her uniform fits you—nearly."

"Even the color fits," Champ mumbled through the wheat germ he always carried into restaurants. "UU red."

Fox heard. She seemed to hear everything. Her dark eyes, lowered on her french fries, flicked at the sound of a spoon dropping many tables away. She ate a chili dog and listened. The food seemed to make her more sociable. Sometimes she nodded or shook her head as questions followed questions across the table. Coach chewed mincemeat and asked her, "Are you a Navaho?"

Head shake *no*.

"A Hopi? An Acoma? Or a Zuni? Right?"

19

"I knew it!" Calvin thumped

Nod *yes,* a sort of random nod, just to satisfy Calvin, Sudden felt.

"I knew it!" Calvin thumped the table. "From the Zuni reservation we were nearly passing when we picked you up, right?"

A hard shake *no.* Not a random shake this time. What's she up to, wondered Sudden.

"From the Zuni school then, right?"

No motion. Coach let go and Champ took over. "Father a carpenter, right?" Nod. "Sure, I knew it from your shorts. Father alive? Or maybe dead by now, right?" Nod. "Both parents gone, right?" Nod. Champ just threw out answers, paying more attention to his Tiger's Milk and iron pills than to Fox's nods.

Coach seemed relieved. "She's an orphan at—how old are you?" No answer. "About eighteen, right?"

Champ said, "Same age as me, right?" She nodded slowly.

Calvin smiled right back. "Eighteen is exactly right. Just like a college freshman. She's legal. And can vote and go to college and—"

Realizing Calvin's plan, Sudden winked at him. "Join a track team at that unnamed college, huh, Coach? Run the hundred-yard dash for you? Anchor our relay team? Score points, win trophies." Sudden paused, deciding to ask a few questions of her own. "Eighteen?" She studied Fox, who raised her eyes and stared back. "Orphan? Really?"

Fox's eyes flashed answers: Keep out of this. But the girl's tongue stayed put.

"You're a Zuni? In that case, why were you running and where?" Sudden tried, before she shut her gaze down. Fox outstared her.

"She's in training," Coach answered for Fox. He was serious, wanting to believe his own answers, wanting this runner for his squad.

"A night jog," Champ helped.

"A distance workout, maybe for cross-country meets?" Coach.

"Right?" Champ.

"Right," Fox whispered and licked her catsup lips. Trying to confuse them? Or trying to please? Or simply trying to get them all off her back, Sudden asked herself.

20

Coach Calvin got down to business. "How would you like to join my team in Utah? You'd run in international meets. We've one scholarship left. Have you had any training?"

Fox seemed to be thinking. After minutes she met Coach's eyes, said haltingly, "My grandfather . . . he . . . he used to tell me . . . 'Here take . . . Take this mouthful of water. Do not swallow it. . . . Keep it there on your tongue. . . . Now run five miles with water in your mouth.' When I returned he would open my mouth to find . . ."

"Wonderful discipline! Splendid training method!" Coach took out his notebook and jotted her words. He didn't bother to ask why she had suddenly confided in him. He did ask, "What were your best times for those five miles? Oh, and of course, you never swallowed the water?"

Fox didn't answer. Maybe her vocal chords were done in by her longest speech, Sudden thought, munching pie crust. She talks when *she* needs to. Says what Coach *needs* to hear. And doesn't say.

"Many moons," said Champ. "Her time for five miles."

Coach pursued the Fox. "Five miles in twenty-five minutes is darn good. Could you run that? Or around 27:50? More exact: 30:50:9? Right?"

"Right," and a nod from Fox.

"Uh-huh. Measured by sundial, right?" Champ said, beginning to catch on to what Sudden already knew about Fox's answers.

Coach didn't seem to understand. He reflected on her speed. "Not so good, five miles in thirty-one minutes, but you're not going to be a distance runner at Uinta University. You're a dash man—dash woman like Sudden. Those long-distance times won't matter." He finished his pie before he asked, "What else did your grandfather tell you—about training, that is?"

Fox's even white teeth turned blue-black as she wolfed down her dewberry pie. After a bottle of 7-Up she answered, as if to herself, " 'Your head is your friend. Your hair, your eyes, your hands are your friends. Your own heart is your friend. No one else. Your legs are your best friends.' He made me chase butterflies. At daybreak I ran up and down Dog Canyon."

Champ burst out with, "Zingo! Send me around Mount

21

Timpanogos after a hummingbird, Coach. Or out to the lake to grab frogs."

His coach asked for the check, paid, and said, "You stick to interval training. That's your style, my boy. Grueling efforts lead to gold medals. Never mind playing around Lake Wasatch." He moved toward the phone booth. "I'll be back." Champ followed, brushing crumbs carefully with his napkin.

Sudden kept watch on Fox. Both were silent until Sudden revved up her courage and whispered, "Your father—your grandfather—did he teach you more about running?" Sudden expected ice or at least the long, cool stare. She clutched the seat, shut her eyes.

Wrong this time. Fox didn't look up while she said in a far-off voice, "Old—he ran across the bottom of a river . . . with powers from ouzel feathers . . . we played the moccasin game." She waited. "Way back there in the sand when we ran under the moon—you, me . . . fox barked my name. . . . Good omen."

Right. I hope she's right. Sudden hoping.

So that was last night in Arizona, a mixture of "Rights," nods, shakes, Zuni running rituals, and silence: Fox's truth. She'd told Calvin what he wanted to hear, sold herself to his team. For her own reasons why.

This morning, in Utah, Sudden drove one-handed, pointing the other from Cosmodome to greenhouse to Heaps of Pizza out by the lake. Coach Calvin, awake now, didn't approve. "Of course you won't eat pizza, Fox; not on a training diet. It's only meant for you. Meat! When was your last meal at Heaps, Champ?" Champ said, "Never!" as Sudden rolled the car into his fraternity-house driveway. "Prime steak for me. See you later on the track." Champ stumbled into the sun. "So long."

"Safe home, all of us. You can drop me at the Cosmodome, Coach." Sudden headed there. "I'll put the gear away."

Calvin said, "We'll show our new runner the synthetic turf. Sudden, you assign her a locker, some equipment. Pull in here." The Thunderbird came to rest in Coach's private spot, directly inside the main gate. Three unweary travelers emptied the car trunk of canvas bags, a wind gauge, an aluminum hurdle, a camera tripod, and track shoes—shoes, shoes, many colors and sizes, strung

22

together like Christmas lights. They hefted all this through the massive center door, past ticket booths, and down a corridor that disappeared, way ahead, into left field. "That's an end zone this season, Fox. Goalposts are up. Football boys began scrimmaging while we were in New Mexico at the Intermountain Track Meet. Turn here."

Into a spacious room lined with glass cases. Sudden said, "Unita's Hall of Fame," when Fox finally raised her eyes from the wall-to-wall carpet and appeared interested in a bow and quiver of arrows under glass. Sudden read aloud the three-by-five inch card lying on some loose feathers: "With this foot bow Mel Minson, while a student, broke three state shooting records in one afternoon of competition. His longest flight was two thousand yards, shot on October 23, 1970."

Fox's eyes asked the question. Her tongue whispered, "How far—two thousand yards?"

"Well," said Coach, "a mile is 1,760 yards—1,660 more than you'll run in your event, unless I decide to let you run the 220-yard race. Okay, so Mel's arrow flew just over a mile that day. I knew the boy. He used to shoot on the salt flats. Every day, rain or shine, final-exam week or spring vacation, he practiced. Fine mind, too. And he made his own arrows."

Fox seemed puzzled still by the distance.

Sudden said, "Two thousand yards? Not as long as your Dog Canyon, I'll bet. Remember where Champ got out at his fraternity house? From there to here is about two thousand yards." Sudden watched Fox's eyes widen, then rove around the displays. Fox glanced at ice stakes that won a recent Western Conference Figure Skating Championship. Fox stopped in front of a collection of foils, and Sudden read again, "Men's fencing team captured A.C.C. title three consecutive years, 1970 to '73." When Fox pointed next, Sudden said, "You read for a change. I'll listen to you."

But Fox moved on from that case filled with golf clubs. She passed up the bobsled and spent only a moment at the javelin thrown to a win at Madison Square Garden. She never looked left at the gilded boxing gloves.

"Everything but a trophy from the three-legged race at a wiener roast," laughed Calvin when he caught up.

"Maybe we've gone too far. But this you must see. Step over here." He walked quickly, luggage and all.

Sudden turned red and hung back. "Oh, no. Don't make her look. Don't embarrass me."

Coach beckoned from his spot near the end of the Hall. He stood by a lighted niche in the gray marble. As Fox approached she saw a reddish gleam on the wall, a shine like metal. Wide as a Thunderbird door. Tall—taller than herself.

"Sudden's plaque," Coach Calvin said, beaming. "She's UU's only athlete to beat the whole world, to set an international record at the Olympics." He touched the chiseled words. "Read for yourself. Out loud. These words sound swell." He put down his camera, waiting for Fox to begin. But her gaze rested on the floor, not the plaque. She shuffled her bare feet, shifted the heavy canvas bag from one shoulder to the other, and stayed silent. Calvin paused a moment more, then read in a booming voice that echoed around the Hall, "Kathryn 'Sudden' Hart, as a freshman at Uinta University, set the world's record for the one-hundred-meter dash in Vienna, Austria, at the Summer Olympics. Coached by Guy Calvin and representing the United States . . ."

Except Calvin wasn't reading. He knew the citation by heart. He said the words while he admired the small bronze statue that stood in front of the plaque. That body had won, that squarish body with its muscular legs, all muscles in the calves and thighs, smooth, not clenched. Rather wide feet and hands, hands partly open, thumbs pointing forward. Shoulders a bit broader than hips, hips high, flat, square. Strong back. A body always at ready, yet relaxed, not tense. The whole posture erect and loose at the same time. A determined body. Determined to win.

And that determined head had won. "You cross the finish line first with your mind," Calvin told his team at every workout. Sudden's bronze head sat on a well-muscled neck with wide nape. Round skull, broad forehead. Snub nose and chin. Eyes with large pupils, eyes looking forward, not up or down, with a slight farsighted squint. Lips drawn back from the teeth in a grin—a winner's grin. And above, inside, the brains. Even her statue seemed to possess one.

Calvin tapped the wind gauge he'd set by the statue.

"Sudden ran that day against a stiff breeze, mind you. So her time's all the more impressive." He tweeked a bronze foot, feigned a punch at the bronze cheeks.

All this time Fox Running kept her head bowed as if she might be counting toes on the statue. But now she brought her eyes to the ankles, shins, knees, waist, collarbone. And to its eyes. She seemed to search them. She stared her stare. At length she said, "How far, one hundred meters?"

Coach answered. "About one hundred yards—one hundred and nine yards, really. The meter is the world's way to measure distance." He smiled. "'You run the hundred-yard dash in the U.S., the hundred meters everywhere else on the earth. The records are usually listed side by side in record books. Sudden ran the hundred yards in 9.9 . . .'"

Sudden pointed the tripod toward the grandstand. "From here to that box seat way down the corridor. Or —from where you stopped in the desert to where Champ ran you down. That's a hundred meters."

"By running on our track you'll learn to judge distances quite accurately," Calvin said, rambling along the Hall. "We'll be retiring Champ's track suit to that empty case over there."

He hurried under a marble arch and into the office wing of the Cosmodome. Oak doors held brass nameplates: UU Basketball Coach; Chairman, Physical Education Department; UU Director of Athletics. He pushed open that door, and the three stepped into his sanctuary.

The room they entered was huge and sunny, comfortable but businesslike. Floor-to-ceiling windows looked west into center field, east at a vermilion outcrop of rocks —Squaw Peak. Books, clocks, framed photographs and citations lined the other walls. Everything glistened. Even the dense rug seemed polished. Calvin's desk, stacked high with *Runner's World, Women's Track & Field World,* and *Trackstats,* felt slicker than ever when Sudden set down her bundles. On it the phone was ringing.

"Coach Guy Calvin. Good morning, Dean Scroppo." Coach swivelled his leather chair to face the playing field. "Yes, she's here now."

Sudden tuned out and pointed to the color photographs hanging in neat rows. "Bob Hayes," she whispered to Fox. "Called the world's fastest human back in 1963.

First to run the hundred yards in 9.1 seconds." Fox wasn't paying attention. She seemed to be listening to Calvin.

"Zuni girl. A fantastic prospect, I tell you." Coach's voice rising.

"And, Fox, this is Wilma Rudolph, a U.S. sprinter."

"How do I know her last name? 'Running,' I suppose. Does it matter with those legs?" Loud from Coach. He listened, then said, "'She was alone and terribly hungry. She ate one of everything." This yelled.

"Note this autograph from Chi Cheng. Coach Calvin saw her win the hurdles. She's from Taiwan." Sudden straightened the frame, trying for Fox's attention. Fox watched Calvin instead. His suntanned face turned purple. His crew cut bristled more. He drummed his thumb.

"No, she's not a missing person. Not a runaway. I called the state police—three states' police. I told you all this last night when I called from Flagstaff." Shouted to the ceiling. "She came voluntarily. Eager. She wants to run."

Fox, calm, suddenly drew closer to the pictures and scanned them. Her eyes stopped on a group of girls crouched around an enormous silver cup. They wore scarlet track uniforms. Sudden, in a dress, smiled behind them. "You—you ran in that?" Fox asked.

"Records!" Calvin fumed into the phone. Then he held his hand over the mouthpiece and said, "Dean Nitwit."

"That's our girls' relay team. The UU Indians. I coached them this year. I don't run anymore."

"I'm sure she's set records. She's faster than lightning, I tell you. Oh, *those*." Coach covered the mouthpiece and asked, "Fox, where are your high-school records? Grades? Social activities? Discipline? Did you behave yourself?"

Fox said nothing.

"Yes, I'm just an old lady of sports," Sudden whispered. "I coach now. Where *did* you go to high school, anyway?"

Fox turned toward the mountains out the window but said nothing. Calvin asked her, "Also your birth certificate? Your smallpox shot?" He waited for a reply. To the dean he yelled, "Come over this morning and see her in action." The phone bashed his desk. Trophies rumbled. He muttered, "Skinflint." He paced the office saying,

"Only one athletic scholarship left on the eve of fall term! And who does Scroppo want to receive it? Some surfer from Hawaii! Can you believe that dolt? Hasn't he noticed we're seven hundred miles inland? The last perfect wave up this valley wiped out the saber-toothed tiger!" He banged open a cabinet. He handed Fox a stopwatch. "Here's another friend," he said roughly. "After your legs and brain, your best friend. Report that to your grandfather." He tore open a closet and tossed Fox a small package wrapped in cellophane. "Now, you two, get ready."

Sudden laughed nervously. Sure, she'd seen her ex-coach almost this angry after sloppy workouts and blown track meets. But he usually didn't call names. The worst sin—dropping the baton in the relay race—brought on his death-ray stare and . . . and . . . but usually not names. Guess you can't eyeball a guy down on the phone, she thought. She spoke to soothe her former coach. "Not to blow up, Professor Calvin. Fox will convince Dean Scroppo that she can run. You should stay loose. Your own good advice."

"Suit Fox up. Right now. We'll use the hundred yards between goalposts. Impressive setting for the girl. Fox, have you ever raced on synthetic grass? On Tartan turf?"

Fox Running didn't answer.

"Probably not. Those Indian high schools have dirt tracks. Okay, lend her Champ's red spikes. They should fit her with triple socks." He clapped Fox on the back. She winced and drew out of reach. "Don't gash yourself on Champ's shoes," he said anyway.

With the string of shoes around her neck like a harness, clutching her package, Fox followed Sudden across the stadium. A long hike. Neither spoke. Sudden wanted to advise Fox, who seemed nervous, judging by her jiggly steps on the Tartan. Hardly Fox's full-moon stride, thought Sudden, mentally listing a dozen running tips from her own five-years' experience. But all she said was, "You watch the ground a lot. Don't do that when you run. Look straight ahead, toward the finish line." She gave that advice only when they'd made it to the girls' locker room.

Sudden untied the shoes, chose a pair with short metal spikes, set them on a bench in front of her locker. She twirled a dial, opened the door. She sorted quickly through a stack of track uniforms, handing Fox white shorts trimmed in red and a matching T-shirt lettered "UU Indians." Later I'll find you a bigger size for your wide shoulders. A perfect fit, after you wow the dean."

Fox Running closed her fingers around the letters for an answer. Her knuckles tightened white.

"Put these cotton socks on first, then the woolies. If you want anything else, holler from in there." Sudden motioned to a dressing room. "Don't forget your sweatband."

In a long time Fox reappeared. Sudden hadn't heard her approach. Who else but a fox could have snuck across cement floors in racing spikes, she wondered as her own cleats clattered along the tunnel entrance to the field. At her side, Fox moved silently, still carrying her package.

"You'll need that sweatband. Protects you from salt blindness. You'd never be here this morning if you'd turned away from the car last night." Sudden eyed Fox for a reaction. None. Where was her mind now? Does she long to rove anthills, leap rattlesnakes in New Mexico? Or hang out in the old Cosmodome, safe from weather and black widows? And with the best coaching in the solar system!

Calvin met his runners under the north goalpost. "Unwrap that sweatband. Put it on." He waved a large, square stopwatch at the starter blocks. "Into them. Into them."

As she knelt to make sure the blocks were hammered tight, Sudden whispered, "He means business. He's brought his Accusplit watch. It'll time you to the one hundredth of a second." She picked up the package Fox had dropped on the goal line, opened it, held the sweatband above Fox's eyes. "Like this, right? Matches your . . ."

Fox ducked and said, "No."

Not knowing what to say more, Sudden wound the terry cloth band around her own forehead and adjusted the blocks, guessing at a distance and angle that Fox might find comfortable. Fox paid no attention. Instead her eyes were drawn to a lubberly ball that seemed to be tumbling down Aisle FF. It bounced from step to step, along a row of seats behind home plate, joggled over a railing and across the fifty-yard line. Not a ball. A fat man. Sudden saw him, too. A lump. Up close, Dean Lump Scroppo.

"Which one's our real Indian?" Scroppo puffed, snapping Sudden's headband. He caught his breath and said, "Kathy, honey, you wear the headdress; she gets your lucky number. Not a fair trade. Make her throw in a feather, at least." He cackled. "Howdy, Guy. I'm anxious for your red-hot event. Little pun of mine, Coachboy." He tried to whack Fox's back but missed.

Calvin called the event, "One hundred yards, to demonstrate this recruit's brilliant speed and natural form."

Dean Scroppo plopped in the end zone. "Cut the red tape, Guy. I'm busy today."

"To prove Fox's suitability for the last UU athletic scholarship to be awarded this year. Fox, on your mark."

Sudden showed Fox how to take her mark, how to crouch for the start with feet against the blocks. Then she said, "Good luck," grabbed the stopwatch, and ran for the far goalpost to time the finish.

"There goes your real racer," the Lump croaked to Calvin. "Kathy Hart. She brought us fame. If only she hadn't quit on you."

For an answer Calvin said, "Just you watch this Fox. She'll put our girls' team on top again." He produced a gun from his jacket, yelled, "Gun is up," held the starter pistol high, yelled, "Set," paused.

5

Bang.

Fox shot out of her crouch. Wild-eyed, arms whirling for balance, she pitched end over end into turf. She lay in a silent heap there.

"I'll allow you one goof," Scroppo said. "That was it."

Smoke rose from the gun and hung around Calvin's head as he reloaded. He popped out a spent .22 blank and slid in a fresh one. "Fox, return to your starting blocks."

With great effort Fox came to her hands and knees. No higher. She backed slowly into the blocks like a horse to its traces. She took care to place her feet as Sudden had shown her. She tossed her thick hair from her face, took a breath with "Mark," snapped her teeth together on "Set,"

Bang.

A whirr of red and white as Fox burst forward one yard, two, three, five yards gone. Then sideslipping down on buckling legs. Fox in the artificial grass, this time moaning.

"That's taps," said Scroppo, struggling to lift himself out of the end zone. Calvin didn't offer him a hand because right then he was trying to help Fox to her feet. She thrashed off his clutch. She lay in her hair, a protective fleece around her. "Get your hair cut so you can see your way off the starting line—at some other university," the dean called from a box seat. And when Sudden came running, the Lump was nearly gone.

"Come back. Give her another chance," Calvin called after him.

"Another chance. Chance. Chance," echoed around the dome.

"Once she gets her footing she'll accelerate like my Thunderbird," he called.

"Thunderbird . . . bird . . . bird."

From way up in Row ZZ came Scroppo's answer. "I'll watch from here. Only one more time. I'm a busy man, Calvin. And don't you wear out your trigger finger on that cap gun, fellow."

"Gun. un. n."

Fox crouched right side up on her mark again, feet snug against the aluminum and rubber blocks, her hair stuffed under the collar of her shirt, her electric eyes set ahead to the finish line.

Bang.

She exploded with the gun's crackle, up and off the mark. Her feet took herky-jerky steps, her elbows pumped a stranger rhythm. And her hands—her hands

30

flew to her ears and covered them tight while the Bang-ang-ang echoed in the dome. Finally, twenty yards up-field, Fox settled down into her same white-red pile on Tartan turf: Fox whimpering.

6

But Fox didn't whimper for long. Unaided she wavered to her feet. She leaned against a goalpost and swiped her panicked eyes with the flats of her hands. Minutes clicked by on the Accusplit watch, silent time as Calvin nudged imaginary pebbles from the pole-vault lane. When he stooped to pick up an ejected blank, he muttered, "This turf is in premier condition. These are the best starting blocks money can buy. Her shoes are as light as cream puffs. She's wearing Sudden's own winning track suit. There's UU tradition all around her. What can be the matter with that Indian girl?"

Sudden roamed the outfield, booting a make-believe ball, thinking straight about Fox. Last night Fox sprinted under the worst conditions; today she flopped on a great track. What's it all about?

Perhaps a fox runs only at full moon: Dracufox. Only barefoot like a wolfman. Or maybe the problem is the empty seats, the high ceiling, the endless maze of walls, halls in every direction. Stuff like that breaks your con-centration. But. But Fox's own desert's as empty. And much vaster than here.

Or maybe the dean spooked her with his dumb joke, the way he sat and grinned. But who could be afraid of a lump? And it was fear—is fear right now—in Fox's eyes, Sudden thought, kicking a phantom soccer ball closer to those eyes.

There to meet the look of a recovered Fox. Blazing cool, arrogant, as if she'd run a stadium-record hundred yards, not collapsed at the gun. Sudden had already yelled, "Not to worry," when she felt the stare and Champ's shoes tossed at her feet. "Not to care," Sudden said, this time to herself.

"Right," Fox blurted. *"Binda beeshan,"* she added in her own language, while her two coaches hung in there and stared back.

Calvin quickly agreed. "That's right, whatever you mean. That's better! Take heart, my girl. No use in whimpering over your three blown starts. You've one more chance, another try for a scholarship after the semester begins: Our All-Comers Meet in two weeks." Calvin took his notebook from under his clipboard. "No, sixteen days from now. My open trials for any student who wants to compete against the UU team."

Sudden perked up. "It's how our team members are forced—encouraged to stay in shape during vacations. They know they've got to defend their scholarships against walk-on athletes. They do, too. Almost nobody ever beats out a regular team member." Sudden smiled. "But you will win."

Coach smiled too. "Sudden did it. How else would I have discovered her? My regular recruiting dragnet missed Kathy's small town in northern Utah. She found herself right here." He toed turf, almost danced toward the tunnel. "Two weeks gives us plenty of time to bring Fox around to the blocks, the finish line, the gun . . ."

Sudden perked down. "And little things like . . . She's an orphan, remember?"

Coach didn't seem to hear. He said, "Sudden, you teach her not to waste motion with that head roll. I'll teach her to match her arm movements to her legs. Same force and range."

"And small matters like where she will sleep? Her locker's too small. And where eat? How live?"

"You teach her—at the dormitory. Where else? At *your* dorm."

"Have you forgotten she didn't carry along a purse? Who pays?"

"I will," Calvin said without hesitation. "Then her scholarship takes over—room, board, books, tuition."

Sudden looked at the almost-naked Fox, thinking how she'd freeze in freshman English wearing a track suit. "And her suitcase? Clothes?"

Coach had all the answers. "She'll earn money by—by

32

typing training schedules for my secretary. After classes."

"And records. Remember them?"

"Fox will break them. National records. World! Have you forgotten about next summer's Olympics?" Calvin asked in a voice of iron.

Sudden shook her head and laughed. "A typist, a student, an Olympian! Just like that! Will it really be so easy, Coach? I mean for openers, look at those fingernails. They'll clobber the typewriter keys, that is if she can type at all. And UU'll never admit Fox without proof from her high-school principal, even when she trounces your other girls in the sprints. And suppose—suppose—"

But Sudden knew that every argument would be wasted on Coach. He saw gold, not red. His Indian girl would be a machine to chase medals. His mind was already at the Olympic finish line with her. Coach of the year, of the decade. Back-to-back gold medals for his girls in the hundred meters: Vienna and, next summer, Los Angeles.

All three had reached the locker room once more. Fox ducked in. Calvin said, "Bring Fox down to the doctor's office after lunch. I'll round him up." He handed Sudden nine dollars and relaxed against the doorframe. "I'll write the Zuni reservation for information. They may send along a complete file on the girl: her I.Q., her grade-point average, her personality tests. Those bear on her training program. You cross the finish line first with your mind, remember."

Sudden remembered and winced. If only she'd used her mind in Vienna. In the relay. To hold—not to drop—

Coach walked away. "In the meantime I'll see the registrar, enroll her as a special student. She'll be on probation until—" His voice disappeared around a corner.

"Until we find out who she really is," Sudden called.

"She's five feet, nine and three-quarters inches. Weighs one hundred and seventeen. Age? Your age? How old are you, Fox Running?"

Fox didn't answer the doctor, who wouldn't have heard anyway. He was listening to her heart, smiling, listening, chortling, putting down his stethoscope to write up her chart. "Superior cardiac function," he called to Calvin and Sudden, waiting restlessly in the outer office. "Pulse next." After a pause he called, "Exceedingly slow pulse rate. But not uncommon for a runner at rest. Heavy training does it. I'll take some of her blood now."

Fox didn't flinch at the needle. She didn't answer when asked about allergies, childhood diseases, teenage sleeping and eating habits. Her dark, set face kept its secrets. "Your blood is rich red—probably full of iron," said the doctor, trying to catch her interest. "This seems to be a vaccination scar. Or is it a tattoo?" A pause. "A half-moon tattoo?"

He laughed. When no one else did, his shaggy eyebrows raised in a question. "Serious crowd! Must be an Olympic year. Now open." He shined his flashlight down Fox's throat, announced, "Still has her tonsils and—what's this? A tongue! You'd never know it! Now close." He looked in her eyes, her nose, her ears, waved a flashlight toward the wall, and said, "Cover your right eye, Miss Running. Read me that chart."

Fox didn't cover, didn't read, didn't stay put on the examining table. She gathered her gown around her and broke for the changing room. The doctor capped his pen. He called the coaches and handed Calvin her chart. "Maybe you can fill in those blanks. She seems a healthy girl. I'll know more when I get her blood-test results next week. For now . . ."

Calvin beamed. "Bright eyes, good coloring, no baby fat, excellent muscle tone. I could see she's fit. Sensational coordination. Great reactions. Those legs pack a lot of clout. She must have bashed your lights out when you tapped her knees in the reflex test."

The doctor fingered his stethoscope. "That heart ought to make her a winner. It will drive oxygen through her system at a heroic rate."

"I knew that," said Sudden. "About her heart."

"Without listening?" The doctor seemed surprised.

Sudden said, "I've seen her running."

"She's running like a jailbreaker. Look at her ragged form, all those wasteful motions out there. She doesn't seem the same girl we found last night."

Calvin propped his notebook on the railing of his box seat and began listing points to be covered in this first coaching session with Fox Running. He wrote quickly.

1. *Head bobbing*
2. *Arms crossing body*
3. *Back swaying in the curves*
4. *Changing lanes at will*
5. *Fingers bunched in fists*
6. *General sideways motions*

He watched longer and asked Sudden, "What does she think those white lines are for around the track? She must learn to stay in lane. And that blanket of hair has to go. I can't see her shoulder movements."

Sudden, intent on the stopwatch and lap counter, said, "Ummmmmmmmm."

Calvin scribbled without further comment. Several pages later he shouted to Fox, "Okay, you can stop for now."

Sudden glanced at Calvin's notes. "She couldn't be all that bad, Coach. She's done twenty laps in under thirty minutes. Five miles without much sleep last night. With times like that she could be a miler."

"No girl of mine will be a distance runner. Not flashy enough." Fox ran easily over to them. "Now, Sudden," said Calvin, "get into your blocks, ah, Fox's blocks."

At the starting line of the hundred-yard dash, Calvin had placed the starting blocks. Sudden backed into them on command. Coach towered over her, calling, "Get set, go." Again, "Set, go," as Sudden demonstrated the sprint start. He said, "When Sudden was training for the Olympics she'd take as many as thirty starts a day. She'd run twenty-five yards, come back, and start again. She was known for her dramatic getaway. A front-runner. She almost never came from behind to win. Now, Fox, watch again."

Fox watched or pretended to. Sudden didn't know which. As she waited in the blocks, Sudden wondered why *anyone* would want to spend Saturday cooped up in lane one of the Cosmodome. Only a track nut. Like Calvin. Certainly not a Zuni. If she *is* a Zuni!

Coach kept the lecture going. "A muffled start can cost you a yard's loss in the first steps of the hundred. That's like giving a race away. Now, Sudden, set, go. A bad start's a gift to your opponents. Set, go. The whole point of crouching is to make springs of the leg muscles so you can blast up, out, and into full sprinting stride as quickly

35

as possible. Set, go. You uncoil by pumping your arms and pushing your feet hard against the blocks. Pump! Push! At the very same time. Set, go. Sudden's an old lady of sports, but she still does it perfectly."

Sudden came puffing from her last start. She squatted and put both hands on the track.

"This must seem uncomfortable to you, Fox. Unnatural and all. You are probably used to a stand-up start. Or jumping off a rock. Or however Zunis begin races."

Slowly Sudden reached her right leg back until her foot met the rear block. Then she moved her left leg until that foot touched the forward block. Sudden said, "Fox, think of these blocks as little footrests, if you want. They're not so bad. And oh, this part you'll love. You get to look at the ground when you take your mark."

Eyes down; toes and rear knee touching the ground; weight distributed on the rear knee, front foot, and spread fingers—Sudden waited in the blocks.

"Set."

Sudden moved her shoulders forward until they were four inches ahead of her hands, raised her hips slightly higher than her shoulders, bent her front leg at a ninety-degree angle and back leg to a more open angle. Eyes still on the ground, she inhaled deeply.

Coach Calvin shouted, "Hold it."

Sudden held the *set* position as Calvin checked each detail of her body alignment. She held three seconds. Four seconds. No movement. Calvin said, "See, Fox, you can't twitch an eyelash at *set* or you've made a false start." Six seconds. Not a flicker. "Two false starts and you are disqualified from that race." Eight seconds. Finally, "Go."

Instantly Sudden's arms pumped hard while her legs drove vigorously against the blocks. She was gone.

And back gasping, "The starter usually pulls the trigger in two or three seconds from 'Set.' But you're not supposed to be listening for the gun anyway." Her eyes swept Fox for a sign of wonder at this detail.

Fox tensed, loosened, resumed her posture of haughty ease.

Sudden continued. "Instead you're concentrating on what you will do when the gun is fired. You shut out every distraction. Like crowds. Like girls next to you. Like the condition of the track you're looking down at.

36

And you think of your *first move*. I always think of the arm movements I'm going to make. Just those. When the gun goes off, I make them. Bang."

Fox tensed again. Calvin said, "Sudden made them for sure," and motioned for Fox to line up beside her. "There's no strategy in the hundred-yard dash. You don't need to plan a time to take the lead or when to go into your kick like a miler."

Sudden took over. "All's you do is blast off and run at top speed the entire race. Let's try first from a standing start—like you're used to, okay?"

"And stay in your lane the whole way. Otherwise you're disqualified. Get set."

"Go."

Go for an hour of side-by-side starts with Calvin's comments on each motion, every tiny turn analyzed, reviewed, rerun.

Ankles this, heels that, no, toes pointed straight ahead, try again, thumbs turned in toward each other, angle of the body so, no, try again, drive, drive off that leg, better, high knees, longer stride, run tall, good but firmer set, don't brush your hair back, control, control, okay, don't rub your eyes, eyes on their mark, eyes look down, go, go eyes ahead toward the tape, eyes get set, yes go go go go go.

Sudden tracked Fox's eyes, hoping for clues to her feelings. Black eyes sluggish, now hostile, now bored, always wary, never lighting up even when Calvin called, "Perfect." Sudden was conscious of Fox beside her in the blocks and lanes, Fox all legs and elbows and eyes and hair and speed, a girl who seemed resigned to running and reruns, whatever her reasons. If racing is the moment of truth, maybe she'll come clean with me, Sudden thought. And hoped.

Then to the finish line where Calvin had stretched a string.

"You cross this line straight up. None of that throwing-yourself-forward business like a smart aleck. That looks flashy on TV, but you can lose balance, fall headfirst. Into cinders on some tracks. You'd destroy yourself for the next race. Wreck your timing. So no lunging, right? Sudden, show Fox the correct finish."

Sudden backed slowly away, catching her breath, wringing out her headband. Her hair stood in salt-stiff tufts.

Her drenched shorts bunched up on her thighs. Sweat ran in lanes down her legs. Her socks drooped over the wet nylon tongues of her shoes. Water dripped from her wrists onto the string when she broke it in full stride.

Calvin pointed to Sudden. "Notice her hands are only half closed, Fox, not balled up like yours when you're running. Clenched fists cause you to tighten all over. Ruins your stride."

Champ's voice called from the grandstand. "Hoo, what's new over here in speed city? I see you're still breaking that tape with your hands, Kathy-Scaredy." He'd appeared from nowhere, so intent were the others on Sudden's finish. In his pressed shirt, satin shorts, carefully-turned-down socks, new shoes, gleaming sunglasses, he seemed an athlete about to star in a commercial. His fluffy hair smelled of the spray already. He said, "Looks creepy."

"We're worn out. Can't help our looks." Sudden smiled at Fox in case Champion had included her in "creepy."

"Grabbing the string looks creepy. At your finish. I thought you kicked that habit before your gold medal."

Sudden sat down on the track curbing. "Champ, there's no rule against grabbing. Not even in the international rules book."

Coach said, "Fox, don't you get started on that habit just because Sudden's scared by this string." He held up the finish line. "'She was burned across the neck by one of these at the Olympic heats." He restretched the line. "Yet Champ's right. Sudden looks, well, unprofessional when she grabs."

Champ pranced to the outside lane and began spacing his hurdles. "I feel like a superfast workout after my record yesterday." He rested the calf of one leg along a hurdle rail, bent at the waist, and touched the ground. His hair stayed in place. "Who's gonna time me?"

"I will when you're warmed up," Calvin called from a box seat where he waited for Fox's next run for the tape.

Fox traced a halting, backwards course along lane two. About half up the straightaway she whirled, shook her legs, planted one foot, took off, and roared toward Sudden at the line. Her long hair swung right, swung left, her hair swung toward the finish. She broke the string with her raised fists, Sudden-style.

7

"She's running like a five-alarm fire engine this morning. Look, Sudden! She's burning up the track. What did you feed her yesterday?"

"Pizza."

Guy Calvin frowned at Sudden. His Monday morning was ruined.

"And spaghetti. Piles of it and fried pie."

"Oh, you took her to Heaps!"

"Rivers of root beer and three chocolate-covered bananas."

"That's sugar. Pure sugar. And carbohydrates." Calvin was furious. "She should be eating protein. Meat. Meat."

"On nine dollars? Four meals? I chipped in some cash of my own. Anyway, when I asked her she said, 'Pizza.' Her only word all day Sunday. Plus, '*Dakanzhu.*'"

Calvin thrust a typed schedule toward Sudden. "Fox will start eating at the training table with my team in just two weeks if we keep her on this. How far did she run yesterday?"

Sudden met Calvin's stern gaze. She stammered, "D— Don't know. Right after lunch she peeled out of Heaps of Pizza. She ran for the lake. Got away clean. Left her shoes under the table. I was too full of lasagna to follow. Besides, I knew she'd be back for dinner."

"Fine coach you are, Kathy. Fox won't be world class on starchy foods and lake water. You must see to it that she stays inside, here on this track. On this schedule: interval runs; repetitions; block starts and more starts. She must not make wasteful dashes around the countryside."

Sudden answered by reading the schedule, thirty pages of single-spaced torture.

It opened with Coach's favorite letters of the alphabet: "*H P A.* The object of training is to run faster in races. To train properly you must run from HURT to PAIN to

39

AGONY twice a day, three hundred sixty-five days a year. *H P A.*"

In long paragraphs that made Sudden's eyes sting to read, Coach stressed the lung-searing speed work that would build Fox into another Thunderbird, another tough machine. He'd written, "Your chest will heave, your tongue will stick to the side of your mouth. You will run with a stitch in your side and cramps in your muscles. You will run on blisters, calluses, stubbed toes, sore ankles. You will run till your lungs take in and distribute oxygen more efficiently, until your vessels expand and carry more blood through your system . . . increased volume of blood . . . hurt . . . overload . . . stress . . . pain . . . injury . . . agony. You will run *only* to WIN. *H P A.*"

As Sudden read she felt her own feet pounding down the stretch in practice, hour after hour, year after year. She felt her lips dry and peel, her blisters pop, her lungs burn, her back crack, her legs throb, her spike wounds bleed—memories of her own run for the gold. She felt the agony. She felt again her surrender to it. She remembered her ebbing willpower, going when she ruptured a tendon, going when she tore a muscle, going when she dropped the baton in Vienna, gone when Coach . . . gone. Gone completely now.

Sudden read more. Paragraphs on weight control, strength-giving diets, meals before races. She read advice on how to tie shoelaces, mend rubber soles, sharpen spikes. She skipped pages and came to Coach's familiar words about mind over body: "Your brain must brush aside all feelings, extinguish every thought while running except about the steps you take toward the finish line. In racing, your mind must always be on your arms and legs," he had written. "On nothing else. Do not think of aches, gripes, your schoolwork, your friends, your family."

Sudden shuddered. What friends? What family has Fox to think about? And what will Coach allow her to think about when she's not running? What *does* she think about, anyway? Fox, not running, who are you? And what will you think of this training routine?

MONDAY:
    Morning: To warm up, run a slow mile
               (7 minutes)

Then take 15 starts
      Run 5 high-quality sprints of
           440 yards. After each one,
           jog 440 yards
      Warm down with a slow mile

    Afternoon: Ditto
TUESDAY: Ditto
WEDNESDAY: Ditto
THURSDAY: Ditto
FRIDAY: Ditto
SATURDAY: Ditto
SUNDAY: Ditto
    UNTIL FURTHER NOTICE

"Fox, what will you make of this schedule if you ever read it?" Sudden mumbled to the tall, cool secret who rested mute against a goalpost, awaiting further instructions. Fox not running.

"She's running a full-bore sprint now," Calvin said from a bench he straddled at the finish line. He whistled. "She's moving off the mark quicker than last week."

Sudden whispered. "She's not moving her tongue."

"I haven't timed her hundred yards yet."

"Coach, she hardly ever talks to me." Sudden tried for Calvin's interest in Fox Not Running.

"I've been putting the stopwatch off," he confided, "until I'm positive about her starts."

"Also she never laughs," Sudden said glumly. "Or cries even."

"She's still breaking the string with her hands."

Sudden complained, "A week of deadly silence at the dorm, Coach. Three-hour gaps between words, and most of them in Zuni." Sudden flopped down beside Calvin. "I checked a Zuni dictionary out of the library. I can't pronounce anything, but I wrote questions—a long list of them. Like 'Where are your sisters? What was your favorite subject in school? When will I meet your grandfather?' " Sudden hung her head. Straw hair fell in her eyes. "Fox scribbled *dakanzhu* on every question."

"The whole trouble with Fox is that she's not planting her feet high on the ball, near the joints of her little toe. She must learn." Calvin called, "Shift into high gear, Fox.

Drive your arms relentlessly. You'll have plenty of time to loaf in the grave."

Sudden shook her bowed head with a slow sigh. "Coach, I couldn't find *dakanzhu* in the Zuni dictionary. Oh, I guess I'll never translate Fox."

Coach Calvin called, "You've run enough laps, Fox. Take five more starts. I'll clap my hands for 'go.'" He stood up, nearly tripping over Sudden's short, stretched legs. He seemed to notice her for the first time. "You, Kathy? Where have you been? What have you been doing all week? I could have used you here in the Dome."

Sudden said, "I've been in that cemetery of a dorm, Coach. Reading aloud to your runner when she wasn't with you. I read her your training schedule, the entire savage thing, over and over. Fox would hand it to me and mumble, 'Binda beeshan.' Those aren't Zuni words, but I think they mean 'read to me' because she listens. With her eyes shut and no expression. No smiles."

"Be glad that she won't talk back! And who needs smiles? She can hear. We know that because she does what she's told." Calvin hustled to the starting line. "Okay, Fox, take your mark."

Sudden looked at the determined Fox moving to her mark. Sudden saw a mystery who never spoke of friends at home, friends at all except once last week on a cloudy day. "Rain is my friend," Fox had whispered to the dormitory window.

"Set."

Sudden saw a girl in the blocks, a runner anxious to please Coach Calvin—the same runner Sudden used to be. Sudden heard a whisper from the line, "Old Legs —Old" something or other.

Clap.

Sudden saw an Indian sprinting, most likely not a Zuni, an Indian girl who claimed that "Old" somebody could heal a spike cut with the touch of a swallow's feather, could mend a shoe—even a track shoe—with a turkey quill and some grass, could run faster and longer and farther than jackrabbits. "Old" somebody could also make better sauce than Heaps by using mescal stalks, according to Fox. "Old" somebody—Fox always whispered the name. "Old" somebody had braided Fox's hair back home. Now Fox wore it wild.

"You'd run faster with your hair cut, Fox. Drive. Drive

42

your legs," Coach called to his smooth-stroking engine.

Fox Running shifted from loose-legged relaxation to second gear. Every hinge joint moved, especially her elbows, when she slammed into first gear. Every muscle worked, even her facials, more expression than Sudden had seen in their nine days together. A scary expression! Sudden turned away, alarmed by the wide-open eyes, black-smoking toward the finish line. Fox, an animal running for cover, Sudden thought and wondered why. Why, Running Fox?

"She's running to save her life," Sudden said to herself, blinking up from her book to follow a tiny figure one last time around the oval.

From high in the grandstand Sudden dogged the flying heels of Fox, noting the lengthened stride, the increased cadence of her steps. Sudden counted tenths of seconds along the backstretch, where Fox hit top speed in this final workout before the All-Comers Meet. "That Fox is no Zuni," she said to her dictionary, "but she sure is a kicker. She'll burn off any challenge from Coach's other sprinters. Rosie and Bucky don't stand a chance against her."

Down below, Calvin raised a clipboard bristling with papers and signaled his runner home to his side. Then he hailed Sudden with, "Kathy, make it snappy. I'm ready for the stopwatch."

"Watch-tch-tch . . ." echoed through the still, dead air of the Cosmodome.

Sudden grabbed her ballpoint and scribbled some words in the palm of her left hand. Leaving the *Dictionary of Indian Tongues* in Row X, she came down the steps two at a time to the starting line. She said, "Tomorrow will be a gimmee-race for Fox, Coach. Not to worry."

"Her hair, her starts, her shoes, her shorts, her final ten yards, her fists, her . . . her . . ." Coach began, pacing the shot-put circle.

"Fox'll blow them off the track."

"Kathy, I've been snapping this clipboard for 'go' but it's too full of papers now. Take these two batons and strike them together. Don't drop them." Calvin jogged down the hundred, shouting encouragement to Fox Running. At the finish line he tested the string, took his place on a platform, waved the Accusplit, and hollered, "I'm ready in lane one."

"Gun is up," replied Sudden.

Fox faltered on her mark, slowly using her head for a sideways glance at Sudden, who gripped the batons.

"I don't mean a gun—I mean these aluminum sticks. They're only the relay batons. Not to get excited about a gun bang."

Fox seemed soothed. She turned to her mark.

"Dolswai," said Sudden, reading her palm, a Navajo word jotted there.

Fox didn't set. She retied a shoelace. She seemed not to understand.

Sudden lowered one hand and read, *"Diinaal,"* a Hopi word for "get ready" or "get set."

Fox ran fingers around the yoke of her shirt, still waiting to hear "set" in a language she could understand.

Sudden read her palm again and called, *"Hihim"*—a Pima word—but Fox didn't shift her weight, didn't raise her hips, didn't seem to understand the starter.

Calvin shouted impatiently, "What's going on back there, Kathy? Don't fool around with that girl."

"She's coming, Coach," Sudden answered, then read, *"Adishni"* and, *"Aha'ni."* Then—then she read, *"Talkona."* With that word Fox rose to set, took her deep breath.

"Diyage bagowayu diyaa," cried Sudden, clacking the batons.

And Fox broke from the blocks in a masterful start, a red-and-white jet toward the stopwatch. In the jet stream Sudden smiled, rubbing ink from her hand. She smiled once again when Calvin called the time—10.8 for the hundred meters.

"Phenomenal, considering she's trained under me only two weeks."

"She's been running all her life," thought Sudden, half aloud.

"Kathy, you time the next dash. See with your own eyes what a prize catch I've made here." Calvin thunked Fox on the shoulders, pointing her up the lane. "She's not even winded. Take five and take your mark again."

Sudden and Calvin exchanged places. He danced to the head of the stretch, calling praise and advice to Fox. Sudden mounted the finish-judge stand, grinning a lot to herself. Fox stretched against the pole-vault standard,

44

did some knee-bends. She jumped in place, shook her arms and legs, tucked her shirt, tossed her hair, inhaled, and finally came to her mark.

Calvin upped the batons. Sudden's trigger finger found the starter button on the stopwatch. Calvin said, "Set." In English. Fox set. Calvin clattered the batons and said, "Go." In English.

Fox went. Directly at Sudden in another flawless start and fierce-footed kick to the string. "Time, 10.76," Sudden called to Fox from the stand.

"Sensational!" from Coach up the track.

"'What kept you so long?" Sudden asked. Then, in halting Mescalero Apache, Fox's native language, Sudden added, *Mba'yen hutas*—Fox Running."

8

At the All-Comers Meet next day Bucky asked, "Who's the new girl on our team?"

Rosie answered, "I don't see. Where?" She shaded her eyes in the sun-filled Cosmodome.

"Next to Coach Calvin, over at the javelin runway. That tall dark one with the almost crew cut. Number—"

"Wait till she turns her back and we'll get her number." Bucky seemed sure.

Sudden helped them. "Number 10.7, Fox Running, and she's not on the UU team yet. She's here to earn her spikes, just like the rest of you." Sudden saw Fox's haircut for the first time. Not a crew cut, either. Yeow! More like a scalping. Sudden groaned.

"Then how come she's wearing our UU Indian's warm-up suit?"

Bucky giggled. " 'Cause she's an Indian, dope. Can't you recognize that from here?"

"Because Coach Calvin told her to, that's why." Sudden spoke from a box seat flanked by her relay team, minus two of the original four. Jill had graduated; Sally quit. Bucky and Rosie remained to run today in the track meet.

Dressed in their crimson uniforms, the UU team stood apart from the all-comers prowling the Cosmodome in jelly-bean colors: lime T-shirts, orange trunk shirts, plum hip-huggers, cherry cut-offs, and heavy shoes with coconut racing stripes. "Clodhoppers," Calvin always called those thick gym shoes. His runners wore Adidas or Pumas or Nikes. Only the best.

Right now he called the first event of the meet as the sun hit noon, sending squirts of light on the eight lanes lined with hurdles. All-comers and UU Indians took their places while Calvin shouted into a hand mike to fans in the grandstand.

"This event, the four-hundred-forty-yard hurdles, with Champion MacDonald Davis in lane one. And I'd like to use this opportunity to announce that Champ set a new college record in his event at Las Cruces, New Mexico, just two weeks ago. In lane two . . ."

To Sudden, hurdles seemed stretched forever around the quarter-mile track. She leaned into the padded seat, glad to be there rather than up and over the ten hurdles that Champ would be gliding soon. Tough event, the hurdles. And Champ's great, no doubt about that. If only he weren't so conceited. If only. She watched him toe his mark, his ginger hair blown and fluffed for the UU photographer, whose camera flashed with a false start.

"Those droopy bloomers must be driving lane five crazy," Bucky said. "No wonder he jumps the gun."

"You have one false start. One more and you will be disqualified," Calvin remarked brusquely.

"Gun is up," shouted the chief timekeeper.

With the bang Champ took the lead from teammates and jelly beans. He beat them to the first hurdle, over it, forty yards to the next, over it, forty yards to the next, and so around his course, never looking sideways, eyes always ahead, on top of the next hurdle. Fresh as a ginger-snap he vaulted the tenth and drove toward the finish. His whole body leaped at the tape. He was first again, first as usual. Then, without stopping for an instant, he broke into his victory lap. Grinning, jumping every third hurdle, skipping in between, changing lanes in a zigzag course, storming the final forty yards, he seemed to Sudden a berserk antelope.

46

"Isn't he fantastic?" Bucky asked when Champ crossed the line again, bowed, clasped his hands above his head, prizefighter style. Clapping, shouts, whistles from the stands agreed with her.

Sudden said, "Sure, he's fast—but he's a hot dog," and scanned the field for Fox. Not a trace, so she put her mind on the next event, the girls' high jump. "Silk ought to take this handily. She's been in here all vacation, working out every morning with Coach. Oh, wow, some practice jump! Beautiful. Smooth as silk."

"Champion Davis is, too," sighed Bucky. "He isn't even sweating. And he wears that uniform like a tuxedo." She called, "Right here, Champion. Sit with us for the rest . . ."

Champ came lazily to a seat behind the relay team, spread a fresh towel on the cushion, and said, "Show's over. It's all downhill from here." He leaned to Bucky's ear. "Hoo. That's Greek for 'Hi.' I'm studying up for the Olympics next summer."

Enfolded in the smell of Champ's Old Spice and baby lotion, Bucky only giggled. But Rosie managed to say, "Stay with us until the relays. Then we'll show you some action."

"From a two-girl team? Takes four runners to relay." Champ held up four fingers.

"Sudden's running."

"No kidding? What position? Is she leading off? Number one for a big lead?" Champ held up one finger.

"No, number two."

"Slowest girl, huh? Sudden's really tumbled from her mighty Olympic days." He ruffled Sudden's golden hair. "Never mind. It's neat you're running again. Who's running anchor leg?"

Sudden kept her attention on the high jump, on Silk's approach and takeoff when she cleared the bar at five feet, ten inches, many inches higher than her opponents. Cleared with daylight to spare. The jelly beans clustered near the foam-rubber landing pad and clapped for her.

Sudden clapped and said, "Anchor leg? I've an idea." But that was all. She studied the grandstand and box seats for Fox. Not a sign.

The afternoon filled up with field events. Calvin's assistant coaches stayed busy marking and measuring long jumps, shot puts, javelin and discus throws. Champ stayed busy as an unofficial judge.

47

He said, "See that fat kid at the toeboard? That's the Lump's son. He can't even hurl a Chiclet. And that guy next to him in maroon sweat pants? I passed him in the tunnel. Pee-U! His shirt belongs in track-suit heaven. Ryan, that new recruit who just pole-vaulted? He's a choke artist from California. Man, is he super in practice, but he's scared sweatless today. Like your Fox, Sudden."

Where is Fox, Sudden almost asked. But didn't.

Bucky tried to catch up with Champ on insults. "Who's that Amazon with piano legs at the long-jump pit? She oughta be in a sideshow. Oh-oh, pass Billy Tully a towel. He fouled out again."

"Those clowns who used to run the steeplechase haven't shown up today. Guess they're afraid Coach would get the boot on their necks this season. Hoo, Kathy, you know that babe in yellow Levi's? What's her event—the peanut toss? She's too small to put the shot."

"Everyone thought Sudden's legs were too short," Rosie said. "And mine."

"Sudden won it all," said Champ. "Even in her moldy headband." Champ winked, feeling mellow after his win. Bucky sighed.

"So much for too short." Rosie stood up and stretched to be tall. "And I'm not so stumpy, either."

Officials soon cleared the track of hurdles, preparing for sprints and distances. The sound of starting blocks being hammered roused Sudden from deep thought, and she pinned her eyes on the UU Indians warming up, hoping to spot Fox.

The mike blared, "A feature event, the men's one-hundred-yard dash, with Intermountain champion Kid Blast Huish in lane one." When Huish came to his mark, Champ called, "Kid, you look faster than ever. You must have spent your entire vacation running Calvin's efforts." He told the three girls to watch carefully to see some superfast steps.

Champ's answer from the chief timekeeper: "Gun's up."

A big, coal-black .32, much louder than a .22, more of a bully than batons striking, or a clipboard clicking. Sudden's ears held the bang long after Kid Blast's victory lap, which she ignored, searching for Fox.

Then Sudden's eardrums thrummed again and again

48

with a false start for the men's 440-yard race, a fresh start, another false and recall of the runners for the men's 220, a fast start as UU Indians tore up the straightaway and into the first turn of the mile race.

"All-comers are too chicken for this event," Champ declared after the first lap of four. "The mile is brutal. Anyone who'd run it has real guts. Say, looks like Ripper has been on the weights this summer. He's even more muscular, especially his arms." Champ admired the front-runner.

"2:06."

"2:09."

"2:10." Coaches called the milers' times as they crossed the starting line to begin their third laps.

"And faster," said Sudden, gazing from Rip to Row XXX to an empty press box to the tunnel entrance. Where's Fox? She's not on the field. She's not in the grandstands, cleared out now nearing supper. Good thing she's not around to hear the gun. "I believe it frightens her," Sudden mused aloud.

"Who's frightened?"

"4:05. The winner—and with a new personal record for the mile, Jack 'the Ripper' Flake." Calvin announced the time proudly. The Ripper didn't take a victory lap.

"Fox Running's frightened," Sudden said.

"*That* girl's running next?" Champ asked, getting up to leave. "I'll catch her at the starting line. I hear she's super-speedy—she's improved those dying-swan dives of hers." He hurdled seats and yelled back, "Are you coming?"

Sudden helped Bucky wriggle out of her hooded sweat shirt. She inspected Rosie's taped ankle, retied the draw-string of her own shorts into a double knot, and said, "You two haven't warmed up. Better to get in some slow laps. Try some jumping jacks and trunk twists. Exercise in place until . . ."

Until Fox shows up. Coach won't fire a shot without her.

"Lookit!" Rosie pointed to Calvin, standing alone at the blocks. "It seems no one wants to compete against the Dashing Duo. We won't need to warm up."

Bucky giggled. "We'll run cold, slow. We'll throw the race to each other."

The two strolled toward Calvin, who met them with,

49

"You might as well jog for a lap. We're waiting for your opponent." He stood, hands on hips, eyes on the far field. The big gun bulged from his shoulder holster. Bucky and Rosie rolled neat cuffs on their socks, re-arranged stray curls, smoothened their shorts, and jogged.

"I'll check the locker room, Coach," Sudden shouted up the track. "Fox must be in hiding."

"Hiding . . . ding . . .ng . . ." echoed in the almost-empty Cosmodome.

Sudden found Fox there alone, fingers in her ears, slumped against a rubdown table. Vast sweat stains surrounded her number. Her hacked-off hair leaked water. Her drenched shoes squeaked when she shifted her weight and started past Sudden for the showers.

"You're ready to run," Sudden said, blocking Fox's path, looking steadily into the frightened eyes of a cornered animal. "That gun's not pointed at you. Anyway, it's full of blank bullets. Not to worry. Not to fall down."

Fox seemed certain to shoulder her way through Sudden. She stared back, rubbing her knuckles, fisting, unfisting, maybe planning a Cosmodome getaway. "Not to run," she said sullenly.

"It is the gun, isn't it? The *ney'atna?*"

Swift as an arrow Fox reached and pulled Sudden's hair. "Wrong," she whispered.

Sudden stood her ground, alert now to ward off a punch or scratch. She held her post at the door. She whispered, "You cut your hair, poor baby, but you've still got your claws. Pounce out there and run away from Rosie and . . ."

Fox crouched, ready to spring in every direction. Her forehead gushed sweat. Every hair stood at attention. Sudden gazed down at the sopped nape, the patch of glistening skin where Fox's short rode up on her spine. Sudden stiffened. Then.

Then she knelt beside the cornered Fox. "Listen," she said. "You deserted your Mescaleros. You busted out of New Mexico. You've crossed three states to come here with us, whatever your reasons. Maybe you hate your old school, who knows. Or maybe you're in hiding. Okay, we're not telling. Or maybe you really do want to run faster, farther. Okay, so I'll help you because . . . because you've toughed your way through two weeks of Calvin's chamber of horrors, and I admire you for that. Don't throw in the towel now. Go out there and win. Forget the gun and run like the Fox you really are. Win that scholarship so you can stick around."

Nothing.

Sudden's voice grew gentle. "So you can get to know us—and yourself."

Fox raised her despising brown eyes.

"So next summer you can represent the U.S. at the Olympics."

Fox said, *"Adan 'zu,"* in a whispery voice and lurched up.

"Okay, so you won't have to go back to the reservation to your grandfather or 'Old'—if that's what you don't want."

Fox was up and through Sudden with a push, through the door, through the halls and tunnels to lane two, finding her place between Bucky and Rosie.

They took one look at their competition and told her, "It's not too late for you to drop out!" When Fox didn't respond. Bucky giggled. "See ya later, when you make it to the finish posts." Fox remained silent. "Much, much later."

"Don't try to psych her out," Calvin said. "She's not used to it. On your marks." He called to the timekeepers. "Clear all watches."

Sudden arrived on "Set," in time to hear the cannon bang, in time to watch Fox raise one hand to her ear and stand up in the blocks. In time to witness the finish: Rosie and Bucky, one, two. Sudden listened to Champ yell, "Guess you really punched the Indian's ticket," to the winners. She saw Calvin holster his .32 and stalk toward the office wing.

Sudden's eyes were on this scene, but her mind was elsewhere. On the girls' relay. She sped after Calvin blurting, "Fox is afraid of that gun, don't you realize? She's trained these weeks without it—only reason she's been getting off the blocks. Give her one last chance."

Calvin continued to stalk.

"Even the Lump let her try again."

He stalked and lectured. "She's a baby—a runner from the neck down." He sliced his throat with an imaginary knife. "She's got to use her head. Mind over gun, what-

51

ever her silly fear." He drew his pistol and aimed at the discus circle. "I've no comfort for her." Bang. Bang.

"Save one bullet for our relay race, Coach, and let Fox run the anchor leg."

Bang. At his own shoe.

"That way she'll be clear around the track, safely away from the shot. She won't have to start with a . . ."

"Of course!" Coach yelled. "Right! Last lap. She'll run anchor. No gun. No blocks. No clumsy baby steps and hind-enders. Nothing but her speed—and the baton. Can she? Will she learn to take it on a blind pass? He looked at the end-zone clock. "I'll give your team two hours to teach her. I'm not going to work with her again. I couldn't stand the disappointment again if she—I'll be back after dinner. And, Kathy, let's hope she handles the pass better than you did in Vienna." He waved good-bye with the six-shooter.

Sudden spurted back to her relay team. She roused Fox Running with, "Suppertime." She grabbed a baton from the starter's table and herded her runners out of the Cosmodome. "No chance to change clothes," she said, leading the way to Heaps of Pizza. Spikes clattered the sidewalk, then pricked holes in Heaps' floor when the four arrived for an early-bird special: giant pepperoni pie.

"Can't run to win on a full stomach," Bucky declared when the table-sized pizza steamed in front of them.

"Looks heavenly, but you know Coach won't let us eat any," Rosie added.

Fox pitched in without a word. One-handed. In her other she held the baton that Sudden pressed there. Sudden ate a bite, took the baton carefully, and handed it back to Fox. "Come on, eat, everyone. We're not racing another relay team tonight. Not running to win. We're only trying to equal our best times of last year. All Fox has to do is run the last lap in Sally's best time—11:2 for those one hundred ten yards. Then Fox'll get her scholarship, make our team—your team." She smiled at Fox and took the baton again. "I saw this girl run a hundred meters in 10.7 yesterday. She's two tenths off my 10.5 record after only a few weeks of training."

Bucky and Rosie whistled through mouths full of cheese and joined the baton passing. Around and around the table went the hollow aluminum tube until it stuck to their palms from tomato sauce. Fox absentmindedly yielded the baton, took it, yielded, grabbed, let go, concentrating on her third and fourth courses.

"Sudden could have used a pinch of this tomato paste in Vienna," Bucky giggled. "Then she'd never have dropped it."

"Or a spoonful of this frozen custard," Rosie said, finishing her sundae. "It's stickier than sauce. How about that, Sudden? Wasn't there any Bavarian cream handy at the *Sportplatz?* You'd still be running on our team, not an old-lady coach."

Fox stopped the baton in midair, then tabled it. She raise her eyes from a banana split. She asked, "You dropped this *en'deka,* this iron stick, in a race? Then you picked it up and ran?"

Sudden's memory of that terrible race was all in her blue eyes. She said, "I tried to pick it up, Fox, but I'd stepped on it, driving it to the curb. By the time I could retrieve it . . ."

Rosie broke in when Sudden faltered. "Australians won. U.S.A. finished last." She looked at Sudden. "Do you mind if I tell Fox the whole story?"

Sudden said, "She might as well know how bad I really am."

"I saw the entire mess on TV," Rosie continued. "Calvin had coached the U.S. girls. He came barreling down the sidelines and gave Sudden an awful scolding when she finally picked up the baton. Waved his clipboard, stomped around her. A timekeeper held Coach back or I think he might have totaled Sudden. No microphone for the words, but everyone in the world could see what he was doing."

Sudden said, "I deserved it."

Bucky tittered. "But whatever he said, it worked. Sudden ran her world-record hundred meters the very next day."

"You quit running after that," said Fox, picking up the baton again. Her eyes smouldered. "Show me how."

They showed her. At Heaps and in the Cosmodome, following their bolted meal, they fed her the baton time after time. Then Rosie sketched the relay course, on top of the starter's table. Fox pored over it while Sudden explained.

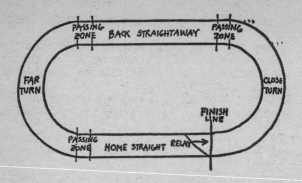

"The complete secret of winning relays is practice. And more practice. All of it right here in these twenty-two yards called 'passing zones.' Here's where you pass the baton."

Fox touched each of the zones with her thumb.

Sudden tapped the relay starting line. "The lead girl goes with the gun's bang. Don't worry, Fox. Bucky will lead. She will run to the first passing zone—there, under your thumb. In that zone waits the second girl. That will be me. The lead girl passes the baton to the second girl. She *must* pass in that zone. Okay?"

Fox said, "Right."

"The second girl runs to the next passing zone and hands the baton to the third girl, who runs the far turn and passes to the fourth girl—the anchor leg, she's called."

Fox said, "Right," without being asked, "Okay?"

"You will be anchor, Fox, anchor for us three. You're the fastest, strongest. You'll carry the baton to the finish line."

Fox said nothing. But she drew a small arrow with her fingernail, just this side of the finish line.

"Now, Fox, walk in lane one ahead of me." Fox walked, Sudden followed. "When I say, 'Hand,' swing your left hand back toward me, your palm facing backwards. Okay, hand. That's good. But separate your thumb from your fingers. Make a sort of 'V' for me. Good. I'm going to put the baton in that 'V.' No, don't look back. We're making a blind exchange. You must not turn around or try to look over your shoulder. That wastes time. Don't turn your head. Swing your left hand. Steady. Steady. Hand."

Sudden placed the baton firmly in the "V," and Fox sped around the bend. "How can she run flat out like that on a full stomach?" asked Bucky. "She ate more than the three of us put together."

Rosie said, "Look at those long legs eat ground. Who is she, anyway? She seems too young for UU. I haven't seen her around the campus."

"She's an Apache—she's a Zuni Indian," Sudden answered, looking away. At Fox studying the sketch. At Fox clutching the baton.

Bucky said, "Champion told me she's scared of bullets. Or did he say she can outrun a bullet? Both, I guess."

Rosie called Fox and walked her again to a passing zone. "I'll be handing the baton to you, so you'd better get used to the feel. Everyone hands differently. Hand, hand. When you're assigned anchor leg of a relay you're lucky in a way. You don't have to pass. You only receive the baton and run like a bunny—a fox, for you."

"Rosie passes plenty of stick," Sudden said. "All the more for you to grab."

"The exchange must be made in this zone, but we'll both be running," Rosie continued. "That calls for exact timing. Run ahead of me now, Fox. No, just a second."

Sudden smiled. "You'll stand here in the passing zone and wait for Rosie. You'll see her cross this white tape on the track. At that moment you turn and begin running slowly. Slowly, Fox. Rosie will catch you in the zone. She will call, 'Hand.' When you feel the baton, take it. Hold it firmly and speed up." Now Sudden grinned. "The best part is you're making a standing start. No blocks to cramp your natural style. You'll feel like you're home in Dog Canyon." Sudden's bigger grin, her winner's expression. "Where there's no gun!"

Fox glanced up from her spikes in surprise. Her eyes questioned Sudden.

"Remember, Fox. As lead-off runner Bucky goes with the bang. Only one shot per race. You'll be starting in the third passing zone. You'll hardly even hear the noise. And anyway, you'll have time to straighten up if you happen to take a header into the Tartan. Okay, after the bang you wait calmly for Rosie to come." When Fox looked relieved, Sudden added, "What frightens you about the gun?"

Fox took the baton and sprinted several laps, leaving Sudden's question to echo in darkening air.

Running, handing, handing while running, taking the stick and taking off, the four worked in pairs until Calvin returned with the judges and timers. He went straight to the Fox. "Don't jab your hand—don't feel around for the baton, my girl. That makes the hander's job more difficult. Keep your palm a steady target. Here, like this." He jogged and received the baton from Sudden in a perfect nonvisual pass. "Say, what's on this baton? Feels like glue. Oh, of all the smart tricks! Red paste!" He laughed. "You're not going to let Fox drop this thing, are you, Kathy? You'd never forgive her."

"Yes I would, Coach," Sudden said. After a long moment, "We're ready."

Fox eyed Calvin coldly. She snatched the baton and gave it gently to Sudden, who turned it over to Bucky.

Calvin told the four, "Today the relay, tomorrow the Olympics." He slid one bullet into his pistol's chamber.

Sudden and Fox walked to their marks in passing zones. "Not to worry, Fox," Sudden called. "Bucky'll hand to me and I'll hand to Rosie and she'll hand to you —we won't need glue."

"Turn on the lights," Coach yelled. "Ryan, you and Champ and Huish and Ripper clear your stopwatches."

Champ said, "I'll time Fox. Maybe she'll get off the mark tonight, show us some Zuni speed." He moved infield where he could see Fox's line in the third passing zone as well as the finish line she'd be crossing soon.

Bucky, poised behind her blocks, stretched to loosen muscles and digest pizza. Calvin told her, "Don't go back to your old head-bucking ways. Keep your form, Smoothy." He raised the gun. "Take your mark." Bucky slipped into her blocks. "Set." Bucky upped on fingertips, baton held against palm by her thumb.

An instant of calm, then

9

Bang.

In a fraction of a second that message reached Bucky's legs. She left the blocks in a screech of aluminum. Her spikes dug Tartan with powerful first steps, her arms pumped rhythmically. The baton flashed in her right hand. She bounced along with a stretching stride. Full speed at fifty yards, she fought to maintain that pace. She didn't buck. She ran high on her toes, chest pushed out, eyes straight ahead on Sudden in the passing zone.

As Sudden waited, all her old anxieties returned. Are my shoes too pinchy? Laces too tight? Will they snap at top speed? Will my sweatband stay put or slop over one eye? This drawstring might break. I'll trip on my own shorts and fall. Oh-oh, a twinge in my hamstring. Can it tear? My stomach is churning. How can I run? Here comes Bucky. She's not bucking. She's in the zone. Will the stick be on target? Will I drop it this time? Will Fox? Will I? Sudden started cold and heavy.

"Hand."

Sudden clutched the baton in her left hand and moved from the zone in a blur of speed. Her sweatband, her shorts, her shoelaces, her hamstrings, her stomach stayed in place. She lifted her knees, said to herself, "Faster, faster, faster." She ran faster. Her stride lengthened. "Get ready," she warned herself, preparing to put the foot-long stick into Rosie's right hand. With a tremendous kick she flew across the zone thinking, Don't flub it, hand.

"Hand."

A perfect exchange: Rosie, the outgoing runner, was hit directly in the palm; Sudden, the incoming runner, slowed, stopped with a broad, glad smile. She watched Rosie breeze around the curve. Rosie ran erect, head straight, little movement in her upper body. She took short, quick steps, holding her arms loosely above her

57

hips. Sixty yards, seventy yards, eighty yards she kept this form. She crossed the zone. She didn't let up. She called,

"Hand."

The baton nuzzled Fox's left hand, missed, stayed on course for the next backswing. This time Fox seized, pulled in a sharp motion while she pulled a fast getaway from the zone. She clung to the baton, arms swinging low and straight through, with thumbs skimming the seams of her shorts. Sudden's awed gaze followed the rangy stride, the flowing glide, then the withering kick and drive—Fox's suicidal speed toward Coach, who jigged in joy ten yards, nine yards, eight yards ahead. Five yards to Calvin. Fifteen to the finish. Fox is running full bore, running like a five-alarm fire engine, like a jailbreaker, running to save—

Fox Running broke stride. She brandished the baton and hurled it at Calvin's feet. "There!" she whispered. "There!"

Then she regathered momentum. She smashed the tape with her raised balled fists and ran directly into a victory lap. Loping stride now. Her cropped hair at ease. Dark eyes came and amused, raised to meet Calvin's mottled red face as she crossed the line again. "Why— why—why?" he gagged.

Both waited for an answer.

"Hoo, just when she was running really well for a change," Champ called down the track. He shook his head. "I guess if you have an Indian friend you don't need an enemy."

Sudden groped for words, for an answer. *Apache* means enemy, she remembered from her dictionaries. But that's not— She met Fox's eyes with sparks of recognition.

Fox threw it for me. Because Coach—in Vienna—because he . . . Sudden knew. She turned to Calvin. "Oh, Coach, this isn't doomsday. She'll be great in an official relay. Just you wait."

Fox brushed by them, running for the tunnel.

Calvin turned away in fury. Worse than at the Olympics. "She's . . . she's," he said, strangling. "She's all yours, Sudden."

10

Midnight: The greenhouse behind Clark Dormitory:
Fox lying on a potting bench, her bare feet curled around
a seed flat. She breathes slowly through her open mouth
—like a distance runner, Sudden thinks, discovering Fox
here after a two-hour search of Cosmodome and dorm.
Not surprising to find Fox spotted with peat moss. Fox
among flowers in this only natural corner of the campus.
Sudden covers Fox's legs with a burlap bag. Fox sleeps.
Her eyelashes, almost longer than her jagged haircut, stick
to her dark cheeks. Stick with humidity? Or with tears?

Crying? But why, Sudden wonders, bending to rescue
Fox's shoes that she'd flung among snapdragons. Why
cry? She hadn't dropped the baton. She'd thrown it and
run on. She throws things. She pulls hair! Fox's own
choice, so as not to regret that she'd also thrown away
her last chance at the track team. And scholarship. And
teachers, books, library card, dorm room, training table—
wow! Where will she eat? Coach isn't about to put up any
money for a relay saboteur. He wants runners, not throw-
ers. He wants winners, not quitters. He'll buy her a one-
way ticket to New Mexico, to the Zuni reservation. Or
tell her to *run* back there. Run along, even if you're not
a Zuni. He doesn't know that. I'll buy her a ticket to
Mescalero. After all, she probably threw the baton for
me. She paid Coach back for . . .

A single bulb cast little light on this scene. Sudden,
searching for a place to wait, groped past wire baskets
lined with moss, bumped into a bench, and stumbled
over a watering can. It clanked raucously. She touched
her way along the wall, felt cool silkiness of glass until
she came to a corner chair. She gouged her shin on a
rung, sat down, and said quietly, "Some feeble burglar
light!" Then, eyes adjusting, "Oh, anyway, who would
want to steal a daffodil? Or asters—or these rusty pruning

shears?" She pried the blades apart. She tried them on a flower stem. No snip. The stem only bent slightly instead. "It wouldn't surprise me if Fox cut her hair with these," she said, half aloud.

"I did." Fox lay still but talked.

"Your beautiful hair, hacked with these?" Sudden let the shears slip to a compost heap. "Why?"

"To run faster. Iron Eyes told me. He said I would run lighter—carry not so many pounds." Her flat voice showed no emotion. Sudden wished Fox'd move more into the light so she could watch her eyes in case they gave off clues. "It is good to run faster. Then I stay here." She pointed outside. "But he is crazy."

Sudden nudged the blunt scissors from among dead flowers and picked them up. "But why use these? Why here?"

It seemed to her an hour dragged by before Fox spoke again. Sudden had learned to wait for answers. She held her own tongue and teetered on her chair. She idly picked daisies from clay pots, pulled their petals, saying to herself, "She'll stay, she won't stay, she'll stay, she won't stay." Every daisy came out wrong. Fox would leave UU.

"It is a long time since my hair was cut," Fox finally said. "To cut brings bad luck. I am an old friend of bad luck." She stopped. She seemed to lose her place.

Still Sudden asked nothing. She ate a rosebud. She bit some strange red seeds. She practiced holding her breath. I've no wind anymore, she told herself. I could scarcely run my 110 yards tonight. But I held on to the baton. That's an improvement. I wish Fox had held.

"When we cut hair we sprinkle our heads with pollen. From flowers or cattails. Like this." Fox reached a daisy and carefully separated the center from petals. She ran a handful of yellow dust through her hair, then she shut down for a long time.

Sudden felt her own palms covered with daisy pollen. She brushed back her bangs, rubbing the fluff into her scalp. She said, "I guess I'll let my hair grow out—to its natural length. If I'm not running anymore the extra weight won't slow me down." She shook an orchid, hoping for more pollen. She looked in a tulip, then in a sieve where she found another packet of seeds. She planted them. She sat waiting.

Minutes passing. Pollen blowing. Seeds growing. Fox turned over. She lay face down on the bench and said in a muffled voice, "You know I am a Mescalero Apache. How? You have a good nose?"

"Eyes. I read your tribe—the word you scribbled on my questions last week at the dorm. Plus you mentioned Dog Canyon at dinner in Flagstaff. I found it in an atlas of New Mexico, right on the Mescalero reservation. Maps, dictionaries—best friends of mine since I came to UU. You spoke of mescal stalks that your 'Old' friend cooks with. Mescaleros get their names from that plant, I read. And you gave yourself completely away when you got set to run on *talkona*. I tried Zuni, Pima, Hopi, Navajo, White Mountain Apache words for 'get ready.' You didn't understand me."

She wanted to keep talking, to tell Fox Running about the Apache phrases she'd learned, the mountains and canyons and meadows she'd hiked with her pencil on books spread in every direction. But this time Fox broke in.

"You did not tell Iron Eyes I am Mescalero." She seemed certain. "Why?"

Now came Sudden's pause, unusual for a world-class answerer. Try asking questions like a reporter and I'll spout paragraphs, she thought. Why do you wear that red sweatband? gets a three-column answer. Push a mike in my face—I'm full of it. Jokes. Predictions. Promises. Records. Sub-four-minute miles for every girl in sight! Speak right into this poppy, Miss Hart. Tell our Olympic fans back home in America . . .

Fox didn't ask again.

Sudden sucked a stem and lapsed deeper into self-examination. Why indeed? Coach of course would want to know Fox's tribe. He'd care. He's not heartless. Why didn't I tell him right off? When I was positive yesterday? He could have phoned for her records if I'd explained about *talkona*. So what held my tongue? He'd have found out all about her. Why remain silent? Like Fox?

"I don't know why." Sudden said. But she knew and knew. She scrootched her chair behind a trellis and shut her eyes. It's late. I'm tired. Worn out by a measly 110 yards of running. It's too late. Sudden took a deep breath of humidity. The greenhouse smelled good—of loam and

61

leaf mold. In half-sleep she roamed her field of memory: Fox leaping mesquite. Fox almost lost to a ravine. Fox running hundreds of laps for Coach. Fox and Sudden running legs of the same relay. Coach would have sent Fox home as soon as those records showed up. First off, she's too young for a high-school diploma. Anyway, she couldn't have earned one. "You can't read English, can you, Fox?"

"I read my language—Mescalero," she answered almost immediately.

"But you speak English. Fluently. And Mescalero. You speak both. Can you write any English?"

"No." Sullen again.

"You never learned in school?"

"Right!"

"Because . . . because you . . ."

"Right!"

Because nothing. What would I know about this baffling Apache? Sudden asked herself. But I won't push her. She's creeping back to cover now.

Wide-awake, Sudden leaned sideways to watch Fox cracking knuckles, clenching up her hands again. Her dark fists swung along the potting bench, their shadows looped with blossoms. Her feet kept time. Her back arched. In the greenhouse glass her black-thatched head turned slowly from side to side, then stopped. She sat up. Light strayed on her quizzical smile.

"Hart, I have thought. You did not tell Iron Eyes I cannot read." Again she seemed certain. "Why?" She studied Sudden with half-lidded eyes. "How did you know I could not read?"

Sudden answered her smile with a smile, said, "You'd be in New Mexico by now. I wanted you to stay with us. Is that so hard to puzzle out?" Sudden looked away, embarrassed.

"He is crazy."

"About reading—I guessed that when you asked me to read the desserts at Heaps. All the other times I figured you were too stubborn to read just because we asked you. No, I didn't tell him. But Coach Calvin isn't crazy. He's pushy and strict and wants to win but—"

"He is *onemwa*."

"He'd probably have bundled you back to the reservation once he'd found your record, but that's not crazy. You couldn't have run for Coach because you'd never be able to enroll here at UU. Dean Scroppo would see to that. Anyway, how could you read the textbooks? Write term papers? Answer questions in class? You won't talk, never mind read. Can you even write your name in English?"

"You teach me."

"But, Fox, you don't understand . . ."

"Hart, I will teach you how to run."

Just like that! Sudden started to laugh. Sudden Hart— learn how to *run?* She laughed and remembered the Olympic trials, her firsts in every heat. She laughed at her own records: state, national, world. She laughed recalling her good medal. Must get it out of the closet, iron the ribbon, shine it up, and show Fox someday. She laughed to think of her statue in the Hall of Fame. She laughed and felt the starting blocks groaning, cinders cracking, tapes snapping; laughed feeling tears starting down her cheeks. Tears of laughter, tears of grief when she'd dropped the baton.

"He is crazy. He used you up. Then he threw you away."

Tears of surprise, a long pause while Sudden thought of many things at once. Both batons clattering against track curbing, Fox's much harder. Dog Canyon and spikes. Guns, pollen, stopwatches, chaparral, Tartan turf. Sudden sifted a palmful of fresh loam from a flat box. She shifted her weight, tipped back in her chair. She wrote

on a steamy windowpane and drew a feather under it. "I suppose I might take a few lessons from you, Fox. And you from me. Here, let me show you how to write your name."

"I will try."

Sudden moved beside Fox on the potting bench. She printed

in loose soil. She added crossed arrows. "These mean friendship in any Indian language, I read last week."

Fox drew two arrows head to head.

➤✕━

"These fight off evil spirits," she said.

"Couldn't be anything wicked in a greenhouse." Then Sudden caught Fox's open hand in hers, traced Fox's index finger over the letters of her name. Over and over.

Fox's fingers relaxed. She smoothed the soil and started over: FOX RUNNING, she printed. FOX RUNNING on a mildewy pan. FOX in humus, peat moss, leaf mold, topsoil. "Teach me 'Hart' now," she said, smiling at her handiwork.

Sudden sketched with a lightning arrow below. "I learned this Indian sign myself last week. It means 'swift.' What other words do you want to know tonight?"

Fox kept printing HART.

"Well, how about words from your records? Mother, father, like that. What do your records tell? Did you go to school at all? Are you really an orphan?" Sudden blocked out MOTHER, FATHER, BROTHER, GRANDFATHER. She said them aloud. "Trace them, Fox. Your family. What was your father's name? And your friend, 'Old' whoever?"

Fox kept writing HART. Then she took a trowel and scuffed it through FATHER, MOTHER, BROTHER. "No father, no mother, no bro—" She hurriedly tamped down the soil again. She printed HART RUNNING.

"Well, you're not an orphan—you're mine now. Calvin said so. Even Champ told me that. All I have to do is figure out how to feed you. Try these." She printed HEAPS OF PIZZA, TAPIOCA PUDDING, ROOT BEER. And while Fox ran her fingers over the food, Sudden said, "Who ever heard of a pizza-loving Apache? What would Cochise think of you?"

"It is fine to eat pizza. Sometimes in town we bought it."

"You mean us—here—at Heaps?"

"No, at Tularosa, near the reservation."

"I've seen it on the map. Who is 'we'?"

"Sometimes at school—pizza for lunch—but I ran away. Old—my grandfather." Her thumb printed GRANDFA-THER.

"You learn fast." Sudden printed ROSIE. "Your friend," she said. FRIEND. "She will help me find a way to keep you. We'll find other friends." Sudden added an s to FRIEND. "Maybe even Champ'll help." She made a big CHAMPION. "Huge as his head. But he does love good running."

Fox didn't print Champion. Instead she thought for a while, flexed her fingers, and wrote BROT.

Sudden added HER: BROTHER. She said, "You remember words!"

And all of the others Sudden taught her that long night, until Fox asked, "Is it time to eat again? Then we will run."

Morning glories climbed white strings around them. Sun warmed their backs. Sudden stood up, stretched, reached the rusty shears. She wrenched them open, then closed around a strand of trellised ivy. She tied it into a lopsided garland for Fox's mangled hair. She placed it on her head. "You'll win this yet," she whispered.

Fox picked sweet peas. She ran for breakfast, fists full of flowers.

11

Fox running on the far side of Lake Wasatch, breakfast pizza taste still in her mouth. She has found a faint path that winds between a break line of poplars and the Uinta foothills. In her easy, swinging stride she moves through a tunnel of leaves. Her eyes scan the ground, her bare feet chuffchuffchuffchuff the dust. She rounds a bend of the widening trail. Suddenly she goes knee-deep in goldenrod. She stops to roll in these chaffy weeds. Yellow-headed blackbirds croak from tules. Lapping water draws Fox to the lake's edge, where she stoops for a sip and prints in the mud. She leaves her mark for Sudden to find:

FOX RUNNING ≫→

Alone until a jackrabbit bursts from cover and leads her, his white scut setting a faster pace. The hare turns east along a beaten path, rutty jeep tracks circling the lake. Fox keeps behind her pacer. They both hurry up. They scoot along the ruts. Faster. They whip around a turn edging an inlet. Faster. They bound down a straight-away, Fox's feet in paw marks of the front-runner. September sun duns them, but Fox gathers speed around a further curve. Faster, faster, but loose, she begins to sprint flat out. She comes even-up on the fading jack-rabbit. It stops cold, turns left, hops for a drink of lake water. Fox plunges straight ahead toward a barrier of box elders.

Faster. Fox raises fallen leaves in her wake. She jumps a stump. She snaps small branches with her open hands. She cracks the barrier, through to open country. She slows. She trots now and breaks a fresh trail.

She makes her way up a wash that leads steep into the Uintas. A red-tailed hawk squeals across the distance. Keeeeeer—rr-r. Doves and quail cross her path. Ooah-ooo-oo-o. Whook, whook. Again Fox stops: to gather stray feathers; to shield her eyes from the September sun that floods them; to watch a deer merge with her long shadow on the hillside; to print in the sand:

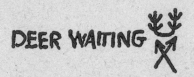

Alone no longer, Fox runs with the deer. Earth seems to move with her quick bare feet. Faster, faster, she seems to fly with the birds. Her thumbs swing high, pointing to a ridge. Her nose sniffs the clear morning air. Her proud eyes watch for hoofprints and bird tracks. There. And there. To the left there.

BAM.

Fox hears a shot. And others.

BAM BAM BAM.

Fox doesn't falter. Shotgun bursts have no effect on her loping stride. She coasts along the ridge, looking here and there for hunters. Slower. She spots a waffle-heel mark of hunting boots and a bird dog's footprint in the sand. Slower. She balances easily, up a slope and down the other side. On a heap of stones she finds an exploded shotgun shell. She bends to arrange the larger stones into words:

She searches further, runs faster. Her legs take her again to the lakeside, where she vanishes into scenery.

Sudden running, ankle-deep in October leaves. Noon sun gilds her vision as she looks for Fox's letters in earth.

CATCH YOU ME ➤➤➤➤

FOX AHEAD NOT STRING ↓

OLD HART RUN TO STICK ↑

Arrows lead Sudden west, south, up hill, down arroyo. She tires. She puffs hard. She holds her sides. At the lake she stops to get her second wind and to find new directions. Here are real feathers: yellow ones wedged in a stump, red ones stuck on a fence post. Sudden grabs these clues and fastens them under her sweatband. She runs north. Her long spikes nearly kindle the poplar leaves strewn along the road.

She feels her feet in pinchy shoes. She remembers what Coach Calvin has said about her "jaunts" outside his Cosmodome. "Complete waste of shoe leather. Racing spikes cost good money. Wastes your valuable time, Kathy, and your energy." Calvin doesn't approve of the daily running, the friendship, doesn't approve of Fox's job making pizza at Heaps or of Fox living in a room above the "off-bounds" restaurant. "She should go home," he says—when he says anything about Fox at all. "Return to her people. Home."

Early afternoon now, and the road Sudden travels comes to a dead end. Not discouraged, Sudden searches the dusty ruts. She sees bare heel marks left. Farther on, trampled brush shows where someone stepped not long ago. A grassy creek bank holds the outline of someone who lay there for a rest, someone tall. Wading the small creek, Sudden discovers a knee print at water's edge. Someone drank here, she knows, someone who also left part of an imprint of her right foot. And her left foot.

Sudden pauses. She stands in these prints and thinks. Then she gallops the creek bed toward Lake Wasatch. She feels her feet gliding. She speeds up, fast enough to create a cooling breeze on her face. Fast, but loose.

Fast and loose and cool.

She needs to hurry more. She knows it's almost time for UU track stars to meet on their regulation Tartan turf. She must be there to coach her relay team. She must show her two new recruits how to set the blocks, how to stay in lane, how to pass the baton, hit the tape, warm down, and acknowledge the crowd. She must show them —if she can—how to hold on to the baton. She must explain to Bucky and Rosie, why she's late every day to practice. They're wondering. She's not the same Kathy Hart as last season.

Faster, faster, Sudden commands her shoes. She knows she's late. She tells time by the autumn sun. Fox taught her. "Where's Fox right this second?" Sudden asks a prairie dog sitting by his hole. Fox has left no arrows, no words to lead her farther today.

But Sudden doesn't need a well-marked trail. Not anymore. Fox has taught her how to track a fox. There, along the creek, many damp toe prints. Where these disappear, a strand of red thread hangs on a young cottonwood. Sudden climbs the bank, aware of kicked twigs. She finds a broken cobweb. She finds a bruised patch of grass.

Sudden plays the Old Leggings game, running and tracking each noon after her classes and before she must coach in the Cosmodome. Calvin doesn't approve. The relay four don't understand. Champ just laughs about the "Old Lady's comeback." Every afternoon on his Tartan turf he flicks a feather or leaf or spider from Sudden's warm-up suit. Sometimes he tells her, "You'll make your name again if they only hold the Olympics on Squaw Peak next summer. I can see you near there from Coach's office." Then he adds, "Your shoes are all muddy."

Pinchy, useless shoes on this gravel path, Sudden thinks, hunting for Foxmarks. Fox must be slowing down, running more on her heels. There's a heel. And there. Sudden finds prints. She finds a disturbed anthill. She finds displaced pebbles, their earthy side up and not dry. She finds a stick—baton length—still warm from a hand.

Fox holds the stick.

"Hand," Fox says, and gives Sudden the baton she's broken from a tree. "Hold this firm. You ran well today. You found me."

Their noon game finished, they run to Heaps for lunch.

Sudden and Fox talking over a half-eaten lunch. Bitten pencils clutter their table; note pads and paper litter their booth.

Fox says, "Wrong." Her head bends over Sudden's textbook: *Sound Principles of Running Races.* "It is better to run *our* way. Out there." Fox points out the window at bare November trees. Sudden looks a question. Fox answers. "No starting blocks in mountains. No ending strings. Grass is there, not rugs to run on. Sun and stars keep time. I find wood sticks, not iron, to hand."

Sudden doesn't give up. "But, Fox, if you run the mile race you won't start from blocks. You'll start standing up in your natural position. Like this." Sudden eases off the crowded bench. She steps behind an imaginary line and stands casually, hoping to convince Fox to become a miler.

"Hart, you are waiting for the gun. No guns out there."

"There's plenty of hunting rifles. I hear them every day. It's deer season. Maybe you're getting used to the explosions. Anyway, if you become a miler you'll have time to recover from any trouble at the gun start." Sudden marks the pages of the book she holds. "Look, Fox, study these pictures of world-class milers and write me what you see."

Fox doesn't have to study. She prints MEN HURT. EYES WHO SAY PAIN. WE RUN OUR LAKE ON NOON. O.K. NO PISTOLS THEN. TOGETHER WE WILL HOLD OUR STICK.

Sudden tries to get Fox's interest. She taps a picture. "Look how tall these runners are—Roger Bannister, Chris Chataway. You can run as fast. You're almost as tall. How did you grow so tall? Not on pizza, I bet, but maybe on your secret herbs? Or on baked mescal at the reservation?"

Fox nods to the day moon she can see through the gritty window. "My grandfather lifted me four times to the moon." Her bright eyes smile down at Sudden.

"But I read in *Mescalero Customs* that only boys are lifted to the moon. Lifted when they take their first steps."

Fox doesn't disagree. She says again, "I was lifted. At the Ceremony of First Moccasins."

"Lifted by your grandfather?"

"By Old Leggings. My grandfather." Fox prints OLD LEG.

Sudden prints GINGS and draws moons on a tablet. She labels them. MOONS. FULL MOON. HALF MOON. CRESCENT MOON. NEW GIBBUS MOON. DAY MOON. FOX MOON. To this one she adds long legs and hair. Then she draws a squashed moon, oval shaped: MILE MOON. She tells Fox, "That's a running track, Fox. The same size all over our country, not just in the Cosmodome. Four times around a track and you're a miler. Four quarter miles take no time at all. Put four quarters together in one smooth run and you'll break every record." Sudden moved her pencil along the oval straightaway. "Coach Calvin's short dashes weren't right for you," she says. "But you'll be comfortable running miles."

Fox loooks uncomfortable.

"You can make our team as a miler. You'll win your scholarship. By next summer you'll read and write well enough for even Dean Scroppo."

Fox changes the subject. She draws a few moons of her own. "When I was born, Old Leggings threw pollen in four directions. With pollen he painted moons on my cradle. He had powers. He knew the eagle. He knew foxes. They told him what to name me. Old Leggings was our best runner. He ran across the reservation in half a day."

Sudden whistles. "Indian Springs, Turkey Canyon, Elk Springs, Rock Tank, Head Spring, South Fork, Nogal. Whew! I've run that course with my fingers on the New Mexico map. Cross-country must be thirty miles. Rugged. High altitude, too." Sudden closes the books: "Yet—Fox, you're—we're running three or four miles almost every day, rugged miles. And we're high here—over four thousand feet in these foothills. You'll be able to outrun your grandfather soon. That is, if he's alive. You speak of him always as if he might be dead."

Fox doesn't answer. She slides from the booth, carries their plates to the kitchen. But soon she comes back to say, "We will run again. Now. You do not teach your friends on Sunday. I have finished cooking sauce."

Fox Running, Sudden close behind her on that cold

November afternoon. They run through hedgerows no longer thorny, past trees that have lost their shapes. Fox breaks a skim of ice on the stream. Sudden squishes after. Dried milkweed moves past their ears. Fox lops off a pod and slits it with long fingernails. The silky seeds blow around their heads. They are closer than ever. They dash up a hill in short, fast steps. Wind whips the hair on their necks. It puffs out their parkas. Sudden begins to puff with the wind.

"Hart, Hart, enjoy your legs. Hills are your friends," Fox tells her.

Sudden glances down at the stopwatch she holds. "What a pace you set! Something like a five-minute mile."

"Not to keep time, Hart. Only to feel. Feel your body moving. Feel your arms swing. They are at home here."

Sudden pockets her watch and asks her friend on the run, "Where was your home at the reservation? Which canyon? Which spring?"

"We lived and shifted. Ahead of hunger. Ahead of the truant officer. Sometimes he caught me to go to school. I would run away to Old Leggings. He needed me."

"Where is Old Leggings?"

"He had no heart for white-man's ways."

"Doesn't he need you anymore?"

But Fox is gone, rushing into wind. Sudden tails her along their new path. Both run tiptoe, listening to what is near and far: To Sudden's feet in frosty sedge. To the murmur of Fox's moccasins in the frozen pasture. To crackling reeds, icicles clicking, leaves streaming by. To the hoot of an owl in a spruce.

Fox hoots an answer. "Hoo, hoohoo, hoo, hoo." To Sudden she calls, "It is fine we run together."

Now Sudden begins to love the trail, the language of it. She smells rotting windfalls in the apple orchard. She feels them underfoot. She hears bees swarming toward hives ahead. She can almost taste their honey. All four directions invite Sudden's feet. In half-trance she hastens across the orchard and freewheels after Fox. Their shadows dance before them, setting the pace together. Sudden says, "I'm still full of run. I'm learning."

Fox and Sudden running side by side in packed December snow. Late afternoon. They wear sweat suits, wool caps, and collars of fir branches braided by Sudden for Christmas eve. Gray light filters through the dense cover of evergreens. Ponderosas spread their perfume. In the distance the chimney of Moondance Ski Lodge smokes a welcome. Not yet. Sudden knows. We can't go back to that fireplace yet. We've acres to blaze.

Sudden's mouth widens in a holiday grin. She lifts her boots in the lightest of strides, slings an arm around Fox, and says, "When?"

"Be patient. Not far." Fox knows the way.

They break off the road, stride in a darkening wood. Ice-glazed aspens snap branches as the two nip under. Steller's jay says his name overhead. I've no breath to say mine, thinks Sudden. This altitude's brutal. And my frostbite's getting frostbite. Sudden forces her legs into higher knee action, matching Fox in the deep, loose snow.

"When do we stop?" Sudden gasps.

Fox Running points to the ski hill, almost abandoned in twilight. Sudden's heart sinks. "Oh, no! That hill! Conquer it?" she cries.

"Ourselves," says Fox, guiding them.

"Lead on, Fox mushing." Sudden takes heart.

Deepening snow, but both runners are Christmas moody. They move joyfully. Fox's wide cheekbones shine with sunburn oil, squirted by a careful Hart, whose own face glows with fierce windburn. Sudden measures Fox's hair in a sidelong glance. She feels her own braids jounce under her cap. Both have longer hair. Getting there. She tells herself: Keep moving, Hart, even if you are a little funny in the feet, almost paralyzed. How does Fox do it in those thin moccasins? And why? Why the top?

Sudden discovers why on the run. Because we're this far, half up. At almost half-year with no coaches, no team members, no fan clubs, no hecklers, no reporters, no cameras, no spikes, no blocks, no Tartan. But no hot cocoa, either. And I could use some help besides my legs and arms—a bullet to bite. My hands are numb. My cap's freezing to my skull. Fox, turn around and melt this snow. No, never mind. We're here. Snow is our friend.

Sudden takes her cap off at the summit. Her crocus-yellow braids fall on the fir piece. She gasps, "Now?"

"Now." Fox reached under her parka and brings out a Heaps box. "Hand," she says. She hands it to Sudden. "Do not drop this box," she cautions and laughs. "Or anything else."

Sudden breaks the string, opens to find a pair of moccasins.

Fox explains. "I helped a hunter track his wounded deer when his gun missed a clean shot."

"You sewed these? Old Leggings taught? Weren't you afraid of the rifle?"

"I am afraid of pistols. How they look. How they smell. How they bang. I have no fear of long guns."

"Fox, why—what's the difference? Short or long, they kill. They sound the same."

"No, my ear hears a difference," Fox says, low. She is busy making baby footprints all around them in the snow. She balls her hand into a fist, strikes the snow, adds toe marks with her little finger. She tells Sudden, "These are your baby feet." Then she prints MESCALERO CEREMONY OF FIRST MOCCASINS FOR HART, the words next to the baby feet. Sudden watches without a question.

"Take off your boots, Hart."

Sudden unlaces her waffle stompers, kicks them off. "My socks are blue, not my feet. They're purple," she groans.

Fox helps her on with the moccasins. "Beautiful." Fox holds her right hand in front of her face like a mirror. "We Mescaleros say 'beautiful' with our hands."

"I like these red moons you've painted on the heels— the color of our baton glue last September." Sudden laughs and stands up.

Fox Running is serious. "Your ritual of First Moccasins. Walk in these steps I have made. Walk around and around. That is right. Around. Then I will lift you four times to that moon over there in the trees."

Sudden dances in baby steps.

And bracing her back against a boulder on Squaw Peak, holding Sudden in her arms like branches of pine, Fox lifts.

Hart and Fox Running under low scud clouds of the next year. In fields lonesome for sugar beets they plow snow for the fun of it. They moccasin down dry irrigation ditches, up furrows, across stubble—all made level by the snow. They seem to waltz, so glidy and together are their steps. One, two, three, one, two, three. New tempo for runners on any field. "New time for your race. You'll run a record mile yet," Sudden says without a second breath.

At that Fox breaks stride. She spurs up speed. She takes a field in a bound, leaps a split-rail fence, and attacks the bunchy trees along Ute Creek. She peels a switch from the passing willows. She spanks her flanks and hightails downstream, deeper into thickets. She chants in a singsong voice, something about "many leaves." Sudden follows the tune. She finds Fox once more. They climb the bank and sit down.

"Why do you always chant so softly?" Sudden asks. "I often miss your words." She swallows a mouthful of snow, waits for an answer.

Fox chants again, no louder. "Old Leggings taught me this, Hart. If I do not raise my voice you will listen harder. You will come closer. You will lean toward me to hear." Sudden is leaning now. Fox gives her the willow switch. "I will whisper, 'Hand,' in your relay. You will hear."

"But when could I ever run another relay? I've retired long ago. Champ reminds me of that at practice. Yesterday he said, 'You're not washed up, you're frozen out. Out of the next Olympics if you don't come in from the cold to run efforts.'" Sudden gives herself a switch with the willow. "When Champ sees my red nose he asks why I funrun in January. He's curious."

At Sudden's side, Fox chants, "In spring I will put Apache magic in my cooking. Mountain roots. Blanket flowers. You will eat for strong hands." Fox gazes over the field. "We Apaches call spring 'many leaves.' You will eat leaves for strong hands."

She runs again, dodging cottonwoods, back and forth on salt flats. Cross-country on golf courses. Counterclockwise Ruddy Duck Pond. Along rural roads, traveling from one month to the next. Fox reads road signs to Sudden as they pass them: GULLY AHEAD; WATCH FOR DEER CROSSING; TRAVEL AT YOUR OWN RISK.

Fox and Hart risk. They run byways muddy in March thaws. They slosh along streams, jostling hip-high pussy willows on their long chase to Provo Dam. Sudden follows Fox, or leads her, or trails way behind, or runs neck and neck with her chanting Mescalero.

"You chant with your whole body," Sudden whispers to the waterfall of Fox's black hair. "That's how well you run." At the dam Sudden asks, "Fox, no girl has ever run a mile in under four minutes. Only boys have been that

75

swift. Jim Ryan and Kip Keino. Steve Prefontaine. College boys or track professionals."

Fox hisses, "Sssssssss," and points with her nose to a water ouzel that bobs from rock to rock below. She studies the bird. After a while Fox whistles to it a high, thin trill. Unalarmed, the bird ambles slowly into shallows, then underwater.

Sudden follows his underwater trail to the far bank. She rubs her eyes. "That little bird! I can't believe it. Walking under water!"

Fox seems unastonished. "Old Leggings had powers from the ouzel. My powers tell me—my legs tell me I could do it."

"What? Follow the ouzel? This water's too cold yet. Wait until May for a swim."

"Not swim. Run. Run a mile with the boys. As fast." Fox shakes her muddy moccasins. "I am certain as fast." She slaps her leggings. "Like the water ouzel. One foot at a time. Put feet ahead of one another." Fox does. "Running is only this. Foot by foot. Faster and faster. For fun. For Hart." With a little jump she's off again.

Sudden is excited. She calls, "When do you want to try your sub-four-minute mile?" She catches up.

"Many leaves will be fine. I will run for your clock." Fox gives Sudden a sidelong glance. "Then you will run with our stick."

Fox and Hart Running in April thunder. Their bare feet take them to places they have never been before, in faster times than they have ever run. But neither think of place or time. Renewed in every muscle, they cover ground in joyous strides. They visit their orchards, their timbering trails, their horse paths, their pastures where cows moo welcomes.

"We're in clover," Sudden says in the spring storm.

"Hart, I have nothing more to teach you of running." Fox eyes a mass of clouds that fuse overhead. "Only about weather." She jumps from their bed of sweet grass. "We are goners if we stay under this tree."

Sudden chews mint and tips her head back for a drink. She sees a blotched sky. "Lightning, you mean? Your powers tell you this tree's going to be struck?"

"Old Leggings knew weather. He read the sky. Thun-

76

der talked to him. Thunder, voice of Lightning, is our friend."

BOOM BOOM BOOM BOOM.

Thunder, like gunshots, Sudden thinks. She asks Fox, "Aren't you afraid of that sound?"

Fox shakes her head. "No." She nods at the sky. "My powers from Old Leggings."

"Where is he now?" Sudden tries once more.

BOOM. "Shot." BOOM. "Shot." BOOM. "Hart, run." And run they do, like anything. Sudden's missed her answer.

Rain stopping. Clouds blowing. Wildflowers growing. The runners beat the sun to rising one last time. Clothed in May mists that seep down canyons, they climb the path to Timpanogos Cave. Their breath comes easily, enough left over to talk. They don't. Instead they chant in perfect harmony. Tunes roam their blood in millions of red cells they've produced by their training. Ideas crowd their minds. Words fill their day washed with sunshine.

"My Olympic races were never like this," Sudden sings out. "Pleasure!"

"My mile—the mile I run for you—will be fun for us."

"Fox, I feel it in your bones. You're ready to try." Sudden stops running, keeps chanting. "But not in the Cosmodome. We'll find a place, a hidden track, or every UU Indian will be there. Champ's been telling them about us. He's followed our joyruns all along. Maybe he's hoping we'll fall off the edge of the world."

Fox's eyes darken.

Sudden scans the valley below, the greening trees, the plowed soil, the lake that holds May's sheen. She sucks on aspen catkins. "No, Champ won't find us. And Coach won't see your mile, don't worry. And no pistols, I promise. I'll bang together two arrows if you want."

Fox's eyes soften again.

"But we'll need timers and especially pacers for you. They'll have to keep their mouths shut. We don't want reporters from the campus newspaper." Sudden turns toward Squaw Peak. "We'll need a secret track." She recalls a town, the other side of the mountains. She chants again. "I ran at Iffley High School once. Cinder track. Smooth, I remember. I'll borrow Coach's Thunder-

77

bird and drive to Iffley this week. I'll run the track again, try it out for you."

Now Fox, a ruddy smear of speed, disappears into Timp Cave, back out with a swift's feather. "This bird has great powers."

To carry them to their valley, where all this time has taken them. The sun waits late for the two who are smeared with pollen from their hair down. They drift back to their pasture, to their tree blackened by fire. Sudden sinks to her knees, pondering the burned trunk. With her fingers she makes quick zigzags to imitate lightning. She says, "Lightning struck here. You chased us away. You saved us." At the side of her eyes, Sudden holds her right index finger and middle finger together. Slowly she brings the two fingers upward, above her head. "Doesn't this mean 'friend' in our language?" she asks Fox.

Fox makes the same sign. " 'Two who have grown up together.' " She joins Sudden on the grass. "This black wood is magic. After a tree has been hit by lightning we Apaches use it for rituals." Fox picks up a sharp stone and scratches 10.5 on the charred bark. "Your number in lucky wood. Not to drop the stick when we race again."

Here they are then: friends who have run from September to May. They've slung themselves in a field of wildflowers, watching the gold edge of sun in the west. They eat buttercups. They drink Lake Wasatch. They talk about yesterday and tomorrow. Finally, casting shadows twice as long as themselves, they run through the full moon home.

12

"Hares. You'll need two. If only we had Brasher and Chataway."

"At dawn I see many rabbits cross my running path. I will snare some for you. Old Leggings taught me how."

"No, Fox. Hares are people. Runners. Pacers." Sudden stepped on the gas. The Thunderbird neared Iffley, the other side of the mountain from Uinta University. "Pacers will run ahead of you and set a fast, *even* pace for three laps of your four. So you won't loaf. Or run too fast, either, and wear yourself out."

"You don't want to burn out before the last lap." Rosie was crowded in the backseat with Bucky and the wind gauge, measuring wheel, and zippered bag. She leaned over the front seat to explain about hares. "Chris Brasher and Chris Chataway—those two guys paced Roger Bannister when he ran the first sub-four-minute mile."

Sudden said, "Bannister ran it in three minutes, fifty-nine and four-tenths seconds. Imagine—3:59.4! Way back in 1954. And still after all these years no girl's gotten down under four minutes. Long time to wait. Decades. But our waiting's almost over." She smiled at Fox.

Bucky giggled and patted Fox's hair. "Fox wasn't even born back then. How old are you these days? What's it been like living out by the lake?"

Fox didn't answer. No one answered for her.

"Sure must have been cold all winter." Bucky pressed Fox for information.

"Right."

"And you've been so busy making pizza, serving meatballs, or running all the time, you haven't had time for classes?"

"Right."

"Fox read a lot, Bucky," Sudden finally said.

Bucky sniffed. "Couldn't *give* me a room over that dumpy spaghetti parlor, let alone force me to rent it. The dormitory is tacky enough. Even the training table has better food. And Champ eats there."

Fox said, "My room has the smell of sage," and changed the subject. "This Chris Chataway, this Chris Brasher. Who will be mine tomorrow? My pacers? Will you, Hart? You, Rosie? Either?"

Sudden, slowing for Iffley traffic, said, "No, I'll be the starter and call lap times to let you know if you're on target time."

Bucky said, "Not Rosie. Not me, either. We'll be timers. I couldn't run three quarters of a mile or even the half mile. One hundred yards is about my limit." Bucky sat forward to point at the intersection. "Hick town. What

79

kind of running track's here? We should be in the Cosmodome where we belong."

"With those vultures? Everyone on our team knows Coach gave up completely on Fox. And vice versa—first. They'd be glued to the finish line screaming insults. Champ would be their boo cheerleader. He's never seen Fox get off the starting line. But maybe if he does—" Rosie grabbed the track measuring wheel as the Thunderbird swung around the high school. "No, Sudden's right. Must keep our secret and use this track even if it's only a . . ."

"Oh, brother!" Bucky's usual disgust.

"Only a cow pasture. Moo. Move over, Bossie."

The car mashed mayweed and came to rest on the vague outlines of a quarter-mile track. A lone cow fed in the infield. Fox ran ahead to stroke the animal's neck. She offered a handful of dandelions. Worn and scattered cinders kept these weeds in check on the straightaway, but both turns of the track bristled with them. A sharp wind blew from the southwest, strong enough to bend thistles drying near a tumbled-down fence along the backstretch. Sudden shaded her eyes from the sun, surveying the oval.

"This will never do," Sudden said to Rosie. "Lane one's all pitted, plus there's not even a fence to keep out a draft. Look at the wind gauge."

"Whirling like crazy," Bucky yelled from the car. "Look out. The gauge stand's blowing over. Let's go back. Not even my Champion could run a record here."

Sudden waved to Fox. She called, "The four requirements for a record try—no wind, good track, perfect pacers, warm weather. We're minus three here. Maybe we'll drive down to Payson High School next. Or to Salt Lake City."

Fox squinted up. "The sun is our one friend." She stopped stroking the cow and began to walk her track, eyes on each pebble, blossom, leaf, worm, and cow pie. Once in a while she squatted to pick up small objects: a cartridge at the faded starting line; a rusty spike at the 100-yard marker; a rotted football tee, pop-top rings, bottle glass on the curb. She packed cinders into holes left over from starting blocks. She smoothed cleat marks. She jerked up large clumps of chicory, filling the cavities with dirt shaken from the roots. She beheaded daisies and tramped down an anthill. She seemed forever in the field, preparing. Preparing it for what?

Bucky shook her head and honked the horn. "It's useless, Fox. You can never—"

"Measure her track," Sudden told Rosie abruptly. "She's going to run tomorrow."

Bucky yelled, "Ah, Sudden, the track is impossible."

"Not to worry."

"And the wind?" Rosie asked.

"There will be no wind." Sudden began to mix lime to mark out the lanes. "Come on, Rosie. Measure."

Bucky stayed put in the car. She wasn't about to help in that wind. "Mess up my hair for a big date tonight." But Rosie rolled the measuring wheel around Fox's track, watching the counter tick off inches and feet. Back at the starting line she called, "I've measured a quarter of a mile exactly. To the inch. At least we have a regulation track going for us. And the sun." She loaded all gear into the truck. "And pacers?"

Bucky said, "You'll never get them, Sudden. Nobody on the team will run for Fox. No one will go against Coach. And who else is fast enough? Roll the windows up. My hair."

Sudden started the engine. "I mean to ask Jack Flake to be a pacer."

"The Ripper will never do it. Why do you think he quit our team?"

"Because he hated his monotonous training schedule, not because he hates to run." Sudden nosed the Thunderbird past the empty high school. "We didn't even notice those boarded-up windows. Guess the kids attend Wasatch Consolidated now. Not one will be here to watch *me* run hare." Sudden glanced at Fox, who smiled and said nothing.

Until that night at Heaps with Sudden and Jack the Ripper. Then she said, "Swifts will fly overhead when I run Sudden's mile."

"And magpies hang around the wrecky fence. They'll cheer for Fox. Rip, it's not much of a track. It's gritty. Seedy. Rough in spots. Open on all sides to the wind."

"There will be no wind." Fox served them pizza and left for the kitchen to bake more.

Rip seemed eager. "Late tomorrow, you say? Five o'clock okay?"

"Really?"

"For sure. I'll be there. No sweat. I've kept myself in condition. I've been lifting weights." He flexed his powerful forearms. "I've run every day since I quit the team. Out at the County Fair Grounds. I'm used to cow pies."

"We'll go early and shovel them off," Sudden bent her head closer to Rip. She whispered, "Bucky and Champ just came in. Mind if I write our plans?" She jotted, "60, 60, 60, 59." She underlines 59 with an arrow. "We want to run nice, even quarter miles. Three laps at sixty seconds each. Then Fox will kick by me and try for a last lap of fifty-nine seconds."

Ripper whispered, "I don't know, Kathy. Your top distances have been the hundred meters and dash relays. Can you really pace the third lap at that breakneck speed?" He nodded to Champ and Bucky, who took stools at the counter.

Sudden said, "I hope I can. I've been running eight to ten miles almost every day for months. I've skipped classes, turned assignments in late, failed a few exams. My grades went to pot, but my heart and lungs and legs haven't." Sudden overheard Champ giving orders to Fox Running. "What's Champion doing in here, anyway? He must know something's going on. Bucky promised not to tell—but he seems curious. He never eats at Heaps."

"He should. Bucky, too. In fact, the entire team. Pizza—spaghetti's full of carbohydrates. That's pure energy and swell for endurance. Much better than Coach's beefsteaks to stoke up on, just before races. On this diet Fox will hold her pace longer before getting exhausted."

"But will I?" Sudden hardly heard the answer about sugar, fats, proteins—a runner's rations. She anxiously watched Fox place plates in front of Champ and his date. Bucky held her glass to the light, drew Champ's linen handkerchief from his shirt pocket, and dabbed at imaginary fingerprints. She elbowed Champ to join her in a prank on Fox. "Oh-oh, Rip," said Sudden. "We'd better get our girl out of here before those two smark alecks pull some stunt. Fox is peppery—or used to be. Once she yanked my hair."

Rip tipped over his Pepsi, then Sudden's. When Fox arrived with the mop they each took an arm and danced her to the parking lot. "You're making us two hares nervous," Rip said, "with all that action at the counter." He leaned against a car, calling advice for tomorrow. "While you're running don't think, 'Faster. Faster,' like a dash man. Think, 'Stay loose, stay loose, loose, loose.'" Ripper led the way around Champ's sports car.

"Chataway," said Fox "Jack, you will be Chataway tomorrow."

"Whatever you do, don't pass your pacer until the last lap," Sudden said.

"Hart. You will be Brasher," said Fox.

"Pick you both up tomorrow afternoon at two," Rip promised.

And when tomorrow came, he did, in a battered pickup truck. Sudden and Rosie rode the cab. Fox wanted to be in fresh air. Rip worried that she'd get wet when a drizzle started; yet he kept his foot on the gas pedal. Sudden hugged a borrowed shotgun and explained to Rip. "Fox is afraid of pistols, the sight of them as much as the sound. This shotgun's a compromise." Sudden counted carved antlers on the stock. "Deer. Four of them. Belongs to a hunter." She rubbed the barrel. "Bucky will fire it. She's driving her own car. She said she'd be early."

Bucky wasn't. The cow met them instead when they trucked behind the ghost school. Rosie said, "No wind at all. No sense unloading the gauge. And look at that— the sun's back out." Fox was first onto the field. The four set to work raking and sweeping the sticky track. At four thirty the sun came out more for helpers, but Bucky hadn't arrived.

Sudden worried. Rip left to hunt a branch for the finish pole. Rosie searched the truck for string. Deep in her own thoughts, Fox walked the deserted track. Around and around, swinging arms, lifting her knees now, running short bursts, slowing, fast again—Fox warmed up. Sudden did, too. And worried a lot. She knew there'd be no try for a record without Bucky as starter. Rosie couldn't handle everything at once. As timer she'd punch the Accusplit when she saw smoke rise from the gun, then call lap times. When Fox passed the starting line each time, she'd know exactly how fast she'd been running. Then, too, Rosie would have to help Bucky stretch the string after the third lap and . . . and . . . like that.

No one heard the car roar up and stop. All four heard the "Hoo" from Champ.

"Hoo! I'm here to start this farce. Bucky sent me."

83

Champ hopped cow pies, over the cracked curb, and onto lane one. He clapped his hands at the crows, said, "Shoo," to the cow. "Where's my starter's gun, Sudden?"

"Pointed directly at your nose and full of buckshot, not blanks," Sudden whispered, sighting down the trembling barrel.

Champ took four steps backwards in his pouncy cat-walk. "Out of my face," he said. "Miss Indian America must be pretty important—"

Sudden clicked the safety off. "This will do more than separate your neck from your bow tie, Champ. Get back in your car and buzz off." She held the stock steady against her shoulder.

He said, "Zippy mouth you have all of a sudden, Sud-den. And your Zuni's a real live one. She's feeding her fan club. Loves that cow. If only she could run as well as an animal, get started and all." He paused to think. "Turn around, Sudden, and see how interested Fox is in your scene."

Sudden didn't turn. She moved forward. "The cow stays, the crows, the swifts, the crickets, the worms stay. You go." When Champ wouldn't budge she raised the gun over her head, drew a bead on the sun, and fired. BAM. The recoil knocked her sprawling, yet in an instant she was up saying, "That's one. The other barrel's for your mean green eyes. Some hurdler you'll be with a seeing-eye dog!"

Rosie gasped. "Sudden's for real." Jack the Ripper waved his branch like a wand. "Peace, brothers. We're here on other business, not manslaughter." He tried to ease the gun from Sudden, but she wouldn't let him. He lowered his voice, almost sang. "Getting late. Wind might rise. Sun will fade. Let's run."

"Right." The blast had brought Fox to the scene. She stared calmly at Champ, touched Sudden's hand and said, "We will trust him." Sudden raised her eyes from the gunsight. *"Dakanzhu, dakanzhu,"* Fox chanted, grasped the shotgun, and handed it to Champ. She said, "Do not shoot your toe." She put an arm around both her pacers, urging them to a final practice lap. Three abreast they jogged the dry oval. "We have been given a fine day to run," Fox encouraged them.

"Champ's no gift," Sudden grumbled. In a few yards she added, "Guess we're better off with him as starter than as timer. No telling how he might mess up the stopwatch. Fox could run a new record, and he'd just kill the clock some way—set it ahead, turn it back."

Rip said, "No, he's not that foolish. We all know he never plays around with racing. Good running's the one thing he loves—besides himself."

"Fox'll show him some today. She'll capture him."

Fox held up her index fingers side by side, Apache style. "We are all together here," she said quietly to her hares.

They had reached the starting line. Sudden stood behind it helping Rosie clear the clock to 00.00.00. Rip reloaded the shotgun's empty chamber in case Champ had to fire twice for a false start. Fox Running hung loose, watching her audience of birds cut air with their wings. She jumped in place. Then all three stretched and bent, shook hands, and toed the line in a moment of intense concentration.

"Gentlemen—squaws—ah, ladies, take your gopher holes—ah, your marks." Champ raised the cumbersome gun. "Set." He waited.

One second. Two seconds. Three

13

BAM.

Rip went out fast and took the lead in lane one. Fox ran directly behind him. She smiled at his muscular back. She wore herself proudly. Her buckskin fringe barely jiggled, so smooth was her stride. Head erect, hair flying, elbows high and loose, she seemed to coast the first curve. Sudden followed so close she could touch Fox's bare heels with her fingertips. Coming down the backstretch she caught a mouthful of Fox hair. Tastes like pollen, she thought, and eased off the pace. Fox must have felt the tug, for she called, "Jack, run faster," to Rip, so loud that she was heard across the field.

Rip kept his poise and his very same pace. Nearing the second curve he turned to look at Fox, to caution her with his eyes. But she was alongside, looking at him. "Don't pass me, Fox," he managed to say. They raced around the turn side by side, neither giving an inch. "Fox, fall back," Sudden yelled from her comfortable third place. *"Edamiz, edamiz."*

Little by little, Fox did. She shortened her stride. She ran carefully, spreading her slowdown over fifty yards until she followed Rip to the starting line again. Cinders peppered her legs. Unnoticed. Daisy petals scrunched between her toes. A grasshopper clung to her fringe, riding the quarter mile in her time.

"Sixty-two seconds," Rosie called calmly.

As they flew past the timer, Sudden caught Champ in the corner of her eye. No shotgun in view. He held the string instead, twisted hard around his starchy shirt cuffs. And he wasn't sneering. He peered over Rosie's shoulder, watching the Accusplit. He looked dazed by their speed, happily dazed.

Ahead the pace picked up. Rip knew what he had to do: run this lap in fifty-eight seconds in order to stay on schedule. He gave no sign of tension. His long stride seemed effortless, his powerful back relaxed under a layer of tie-dyed cotton. Not wet yet, Sudden realized, noticing her own sweatband hot and sopping. He's still full of run. So was Fox, whose feet sent dandelion fluff right and left along the curve.

So was Sudden full of run. Sweat but no sweat. She glided like a specter through that late day. No bouncing, no bounding. No unnecessary head or trunk or waist movements that would burn oxygen she'd need for the next lap. Down the backstretch she stayed loose, loose, loose, feeling her own strength. Rip's strength, Fox's. The three gave in to the sweet hypnosis of running. All life was in motion, not them. Mountains seemed to tremble on the horizon. Mare's-tail clouds blew there, too. In middle distance a raven spoke from his telephone pole. Cr-r-ruk. Closer up the cow munched dinner at the edge of the second turn. Runners rounding it passed her unobserved. They sprinted for the timer. Mountains, raven, cow stayed put.

"2:02.1," Rosie called, excitedly.

"2:02.1," Champ echoed.

"2:02.1," Sudden said to herself. Only an instant to spy on Champ. There, he's grinning at the Accusplit. And right here, at the beginning of lap three, I must take over as pacer.

Sudden made her move on time. She kicked into lane two, rode Fox's hip briefly, then squirted past her and into lane one. She ran behind Rip. She backfired cinders and said, *"Wfa'ail,"* to his high-flying elbows. Rip heard her. Without a hitch he swung out to lane two, three, four, and off the track at the first turn. He bent double and gulped air, a winded spectator now instead of a Chris Chataway. He watched the other hare take over.

Sudden sprang into the lead with the confident steps of a Chris Brasher. She used her arms, lifted high her knees to set a wicked pace—one that would recapture the two seconds they'd lost on the first lap. She whirled the curve. She told herself faster, looser, faster, looser. She surged along the straightaway, ponytail spanking her shoulder blades. Faster. Faster. Total concentration. Sudden ignored familiar landmarks flowing by. She kept her eyes leveled on the dirt ten feet ahead and listened only for Fox's feet behind. No feet! Instead she heard her own labored breathing, her own blood thumping in her ears. Faster. She felt her tongue dry to the tips of her teeth, felt her knees turn out, her hands got too high. "Kathy, you're losing form." Her own voice? No, Champ's, somewhere around the second bend! "Loose. Loose," he called excitedly. No insults, only help.

And where was Fox's voice? Where was she, anyway, Sudden wondered. No other panting, no footfalls but her own on the track. No time to glance behind. Sudden's body ached. Her legs weighed a ton apiece. She seemed to be suffocating, as if she'd run a thousand miles already, not the thousand yards she'd really come. She felt herself tightening more. She felt—

Just then the low evening sun sent a shadow forward into Sudden's path. Fox! Running easily, there she was, stretched forever in front of the fading pacesetter. Sudden felt her hair break into waves. She felt her breath flood back. She dropped her arms at full length for two strides and loosened her back. She felt speed and spring reviving in her legs. She regained her form, smooth and strong. She accelerated against her body's pain. Her feet caught fire; her legs ate the cinders. She bore down on the timer, who waved a handkerchief madly at the line.

"3:00.5! Unbelievable!" Champ called. Sudden had never heard him so excited, not even by his own track records.

3:00.5, Sudden thought, jumping the curb to the infield without breaking stride. She buckled at the waist. She gasped and staggered. She coughed her tongue loose from where it stuck to the inside of her cheek. After that she braced up to watch Fox take over on her difficult last lap. No pacers now. Or competition to spur her. A solo run. Nothing but voices behind, farther behind, way behind.

"Be mean! Hang tough!" Champ called, his first words of encouragement to Fox.

Relax, thought Sudden.

"Go after that record," Rip hollered from the first turn. He twirled his shirt above his head and tossed it down as Fox flashed by. "You're still strong—strong. Don't let the bear jump on your back," he screamed after her.

"Stay with it. Put out. Bring it in." Champ waved his linen handkerchief and dropped it with a flourish, a signal for record time going into the final lap. He unwound the finish string with one hand. His other held the stopwatch he'd wrestled from Rosie. His eyes never left Fox. He kept saying, "Oh, she's speedy—she's super—she's beautif—"

Rosie met Sudden's look about the watch. I couldn't help it, she seemed to say.

But Sudden knew that Champ was on their side now. "Not to worry," she whispered, her breath returning.

For ten seconds, then gone again when Fox stumbled on the far straightaway. Stumbled, threw both arms forward protectively, jerked earthward, nearly toppled, spun right, lurched into lane two—but didn't nose-dive. She planted her left foot, caught herself on the way down, upped her arms, up, upped her shoulders, up, upped her chin.

"Oh, Fox," Sudden breathed.

"Fox Running. Fox Running," Rip called with all his might.

"Nowhere, no way she can do it now," Champ howled, while seconds clicked in his sweaty hand. Two tears slid sideways out of Rosie's eyes. Champ let the finish line dangle, but Rosie snatched it, pulled it taut across the lanes. Champ sniffed back a tear.

Feet almost at a standstill, Fox fought to recover her balance. Then she tilted and tipped for five yards, until life seemed to flow back to her limbs. She cut loose once more, ran free. In another fifteen yards she'd regained her form. She gathered speed. More. More. She sprinted stubbornly but gracefully, Fox Running down a corridor of time that curved one last curve toward the unremitting Accusplit. With two hundred yards to go, she lengthened her beautiful stride. Scenery seemed to flee backwards, away from her thunderbolt kick: mountains changed to anthills; clouds became dots; crows turned to hummingbirds. The track shuddered under her pounding feet. She streaked down the homestretch as never before.

"Relax. Relax."

"Hold your form." Champ wasn't crying now. "Fox. Foxxxxxxxx." He gagged for joy.

Red legs flashing in cahoots with her arms, Fox blazed the final fifty. Rivulets of sweat stained her face. Pollen dripped from her earlobes. Yet she hung cool, smooth, deadly swift on target. Sunshine arrows lit her trail to the finish.

"Run through the tape."

"Smash it."

Couldn't be heard over the screaming, leaping Champ. "You can do it all," he finally managed to blurt, and he mashed the stop button as Fox caught the string with open hands.

Fox kept running, but slowly, slower, even more. She dropped her hands to her hips. She leaned forward, coughed and coughed, choked until Sudden caught up with her and slapped her on the back. They hung together in the middle of the track. They listened to Champ, who tried to say, "Ladies and Gentlemen," but said, "Gen—dell—umps," in his excitement.

"Gen—dell—umps. Announcing the winner of the one-mile record try, Number—she has no number. But she has a name: Fox Running, Running for the Uinta University Indians, no, running for, for . . ."

"For herself," Rip declared.

"Herself, running for herself with a time that is a new record for this track, a new record for American women,

89

a new world record for women, a racing milestone. The time of 3 . . ."

Rosie shrieked over the rest of that sentence. Rip started ripping up daisies.

"3," Champ tried, but the cow's moo did him in.

Sudden felt tears start. She said, "You are the one," to Fox and wrapped her in a beach towel.

"3:59.9 Whew!" Champ sang and danced in a circle. "You're the champ, you're our champ."

The sun had gone by the time all their dancing was done. When night hawks replaced swifts over the infield, the five athletes hooked arms and sauntered around their track in a record-slow victory lap. No one spoke for the longest time. A million *whoopies* had wrecked their throats. Finally Rip said, "Hand," on the backstretch and presented Fox with a bouquet of daisies. She fed it to the cow, all but one flower. She pulled a petal with each slow step, ending with, "She'll stay," whispered to Sudden.

"She'll stay and she'll run in the Olympics," whispered back.

Coming to the wire, Champ found his voice. "Hey, I had it all wrong about— Good thing me and Sudden caught you on the desert! Say, Fox, are there any other orphans like you down on the Zuni reservation?"

"*Ha-waka.*"

"What's she saying?" Champ really wanted to know.

"That's Mescalero Apache for 'Your shirt is dirty,' Champ."

Champion looked at himself, all covered with cinders and grass and who-knows-what from their grubby, magic track at Iffley. He didn't brush or fluff his hair or straighten his gone-awry tie. He said only "3:59.9," to the dusk.

14

"3:59.9?"

"Precisely what I said, Coach Calvin. I've told you three times now." Sudden smiled at Calvin's startled voice. "Here's your Accusplit back. See for yourself." She slid the stopwatch across his desk.

Calvin's fingers automatically closed, but he didn't even glance at the numbers. He didn't go for his glasses, either. He tilted his chair, sipped a can of iced tea, and stared out the window toward Squaw Peak. He whistled. "3:59.9!" He tilted more. "A gold medal."

Sudden said, "Easily."

The chair snapped Calvin forward again. "In the *second* place, I don't believe it, Kathy. The girl may be fast —okay, we know this. Yet—yet to break a record with bare feet on dirt, with a quitter like Jack Flake as pacer. And you? You've no experience with the half mile, let alone three quarters. How could . . . and you've hardly run at all this year. A few daily laps with your relay team and chasing around with Fox in the hills."

"Eight fast miles a day lately—sometimes more—isn't exactly messing around, Coach. It's training on a schedule. Just like yours, only outdoors, all different times. Dawn. Noons. Nights even. You should see the moon—"

"Funrunning!" Calvin harrumphed.

"Sure, we've had fun. Plus we've built up our wind, our lungs, our hearts, our legs, our—"

"Nonsense!" Calvin said, sure of himself as usual. "Pain is gain. Pain."

Sudden looked him squarely in the eyes. "Fox brought me around to running again, showed me it's chanting with my body. She taught me on her schedule, her grounds. She's proved it can be fun."

Calvin swiveled around fast. He clicked the stopwatch back to zero, held it up. "There's her world record. Her

WR! Zero!" He raced his fingers through his hair. "In the first place, suppose she did run sub-four. Of course it doesn't count on that unmeasured track."

"Rosie measured. She'll tell you."

"With all kinds of wind assistance."

"Zero wind. The only zero yesterday."

Calvin tried again. "Downhill, for all the official record books would know."

"Level, quarter-mile oval. Up at Iffley. You've seen that track. And it was completely windless yesterday. Five witnesses, including Champion MacDonald Davis, are prepared to swear on a stack—"

Guy Calvin rolled around. "Champ was there? He didn't tell me." Calvin looked at one of the eleven clocks ticking around his glassed-in sanctuary. He reached for the intercom, buzzed his secretary. He told her, "Call Champion Davis in the weight room. Right now." To Sudden he said, "That record doesn't count because you needed three official timers to compare watches and an official .32 caliber for starts. Say, what did you do about a gun? Her sub-four include the infamous floundering at the start?"

"Fox started—"

"Perfectly," said Champ at the door. "Those shotgun pellets I fired are still landing. Pow. Pow. Take that and that." Champ cocked his wrists. He squinted along his imaginary gun. "Pelting the worm burrows."

"She ran on worms?"

"Or falling on the cow and magpies, poor critters." Sudden saluted Champ. "Both shells were blanks."

Calvin looked at his two students as if they'd gone crazy. "Worms? Birds? What sort of running track could that be? Next you'll confess that you saw a—"

"Fox Running," Champ boomed with pleasure, then blurted out the eintire story from his point of view, including why he was there at all: Bucky had told him about the secret race and then was afraid to show up with him. He was full of praise for Fox. No put-downs today. He ended with, "Hoo, would have been 3:58.9 maybe if she hadn't stumbled on a prairie-dog hole. Or maybe not. She seems to run harder when she's had trouble. She's some athlete!"

And Sudden threw in, "Thus they lived happily ever after with a new world record."

Calvin deserted his chair. "A WR that we can't submit to the A.A.U., the I.C.4-A, the N.C.A.A., the USTFP, the I.T.A. professional tour, *Women's Track & Field Annual.* Not even the Iffley newspaper will print such a myth."

"It's no myth, Coach. She broke the four-minute barrier. I'll testify," Champ promised, and grinned at Sudden.

Calvin paced the carpet in giant steps while muttering, "Imagine. Another WR right here at Uinta. Well, at least nearby. But who's to believe it?" At the trophy case he rocked back on his heels, looked out the window, and said, "If only I'd been there! Why didn't you— If only you'd announced the race, made the whole thing public, invited some other milers to compete—out-of-state girls. Then we'd have a world record. Blast it! If only . . . timers . . . starters . . . judges . . wind . . . guns . . ."

Sudden stopped listening to remember her years of "if only." She used to say it every day in her running career. If only I hadn't been assigned lane five for this race. If only the blocks had been set farther forward. If only we were running at sea level I'd have more oxygen. If only the track weren't so spongy. If only I hadn't melted in a puddle of sweat . . . blood . . . nerves . . . inflamed tendons . . . broken straps . . . missed breakfasts . . . falling batons. Sudden thought of her own blistering laps at Iffley. She thought of Fox, and she knew the "if only's" were all in the past. Sudden was sure right then she'd come out of retirement. She knew she'd race again. She believed she'd win again.

Calvin asked loud and clear, "Who's going to believe that an unranked, unknown Zuni Indian girl—"

"Mescalero," Champ corrected. "One of the Apache tribes. They tied their enemies to anthills." Sudden caught his eye. "At least in the movies," he added. "Probably all made up."

"A Mescalero foundling—eighteen years old," Calvin continued.

Sudden didn't correct him about Fox's age. Why complicate matters just now? Instead she looked straight at the biggest trophy on his wall—hers—and interrupted with, "Do you believe me about 3:59.9? Do you believe in Fox?"

"Yes, I believe you," he said at once. Nothing more until he'd traveled from bookcases to files to photos to

93

his swivel chair. He dropped heavily into it. He polished a plaque with his shirt sleeve. He flipped open the *Guinness Book of World Records,* scribbled in the margin. Sudden couldn't see what. "Yes," he said again. "And I believe in her, in Fox Running. That girl can run the legs off a moose when she wants to. When *she* wants to." He winked up at his two champions. "She throws a pretty mean baton, too."

Back of that wink, what? Had he forgiven Fox her gun-shy starts, her sudden change of heart in his All-Comers Meet? Had he forgotten her dismal trial as his dash girl? Did he understand why Sudden ran after Fox on that August day last year, hung with Fox all winter, trained with her until May, ran hare for her yesterday in the world's most obscure mile race, with his stopwatch? Had he forgiven Sudden, finally, three years, nine months later, forgotten the thunderclap of her baton on the curb in Vienna?

Forgive? Understand? Forget? Sudden meant to find out.

She asked, "So you'll help her run—help us? We need you. I want her—Fox feels—we both hope she can enter the trials the end of next month and win there, then go on to the Olympics in August. This time we'll leave nothing to 'if' about. She will win."

Now there was a long pause.

Champ tried isometric exercises in his straight-backed chair and counted Sudden's trophies. Sudden scanned the mountains and ran races in her head: her own Olympic trials, all three heats in a record July heat wave. She'd never been that wet before. Just remembering, she reached for her sweatband. Lucky for Fox she can tolerate any weather. No, not luck. She understands weather. She's lived outdoors all her life. Weather is her friend, her magic. Fox will take a gold medal under the late-summer sun of Los Angeles, *if* she runs there.

Sudden exchanged a glance with Champ, raised eyebrows asking, "Will Coach do it?" She turned her eager face to meet the answer.

With a hand covering his eyes, Calvin put forth the reasons why not.

"Tactics make a miler, not sheer leg speed. Fox knows nothing of running in a pack or setting a pace or coming from behind. She'd be elbowed off any track at the first

94

turn or maybe lured into a fistfight and disqualified. We're not sure—you don't know and I doubt if she does —if she's a front-runner or a wait-and-kick type. She might want to lead the pack and then tire out on the first or second lap. Or she might wait too long to come from behind."

"You should have seen her kick the final two-twenty toward me yesterday, Coach. She had plenty of juice left." Champ skated his fingers along the desk top.

Calvin resisted even his Champ. "She had juice left because of Kathy and Jack. They kept her from running herself out in the first three laps. But who's going to pace her at the trials? Seasoned milers will beat her with tactics."

Champ said, "She'll learn to outfox them. I'll teach her. I'll read up on miling strategy. I'll show her my elbows."

Calvin lifted his eyes, contemplating his shelf of starter's pistols. "Then there's her starts to worry about. The gun. No one falls down in a major race and survives. And I doubt if the Olympic committee would agree to a shotgun-blast start. Our girl will lie in Tartan while Miss Guld breezes past the body. Or Cheryl Gibbons jumps her. Or Robin Minty tromples all over her."

"Hoo, that Minty. She'd give her own grandmother a face full of knuckles to keep her from winning. She's got a smart mouth, too. She reminds me of me."

"We won't let Gibbons scare us, Coach. I saw her run at Madison Square Garden last year when you sent me with the relay team. She's a regular windmill. Flails her arms, rolls her head, shakes her hips. No style at all."

Champ said, "I heard she's not too bright. She'll never be international without brains. You run with your head, right, Coach?"

Calvin opened a cabinet, took out a fat ring binder marked *Scouting Reports*. He read aloud from it: "Gibbons, Cheryl: 5′5″, weight 115, age 17, ran a 4:15 mile at Irvine, California, outdoors; ran a 4:16 indoors at Philadelphia, 4:11 at Houston.' Windmill or not, nitwit or not, she wins."

"Fox will blow by her," Champ promised.

"And 'Minty, Robin: 5′6″, weight 109, age 19, ran second at Irvine, first at Richmond against the Russians, disqualified in Oregon, best time of 4:10 this year.' I'd rate

95

her right behind Guld as the likeliest U.S. prospect for a first."

"Fox is the likeliest," was all Sudden said.

Coach wrote something carefully on that page, pushed his notebook to Sudden. "In any case, this list is endless with nifty runners—tacticians, big kickers, polished veterans, hungry little girls figuring to represent us at Los Angeles. Take your pick. Fox would be in trouble."

Sudden picked up the notebook. She thought, Whew, this is heavy all right. Even the names look speedy: Barbi, Francie, Jackie, Julie, Nancy, Trina, Toni, Wendy. All of them with years of indoor/outdoor miles. Experienced up to the hilt.

Beginning at the bottom of the open page, Sudden read up the United States milers. Their best times: 4:21, 4:19, 4:16, right up to 4:07. Their heights and weights: 5'4", 5'11", 103 pounds, 123 lbs. Their track teams and colleges: Cindergals, Tigerettes, Wills Spikettes, San Jose State, Tennessee State, University of Ohio. She read right up to the brightest star, who was third at Denver, second at Yale, first at Miami, at Berkeley, at Phoenix, with times of 4:09, 4:10, 4:07—first: Shelly "Guld" Eberly. Taller than Fox. Best girl miler on earth. Until Fox. Guld had won the gold medal in Vienna. Sudden had seen her uncork the greatest finish of any event in the *Sportsplatz*—greatest finish until Iffley.

But there, above Guld's name in the notebook, Coach had printed, "Fox Running, 5'9 3/4", 117, Iffley, 3.59.9, 1st. She competes unattached to any university or track club."

Sudden grinned a winner's grin. She wrote,

RUNS FOR HERSELF, FOR FUN →

and drew a big arrow. She said, "If Guld hears those foxfeet padding up on her she'll sidle off the track in panic. Will you help us, Coach? Will you enter Fox in the trials? Will you take her along when we drive down to Tucson? Will you?"

Still Calvin sat without a promise.

Sudden hunkered down to wait him out, a trick she'd

learned from Fox. Champ had no more words to say. He squirmed and put the whammy on Coach, his green eyes full of "do it."

After a world-record silence Calvin mumbled, "She'd have to train hard, not play around the lake. Train to compete. No solo runner—no matter how fast—can go up against that strong field without tactics." He narrowed his gray eyes. "The girl would make any coach in America jump from bleachers. She's been so unpredictable, so silent, so strange about the gun, so—so—so—"

"Swift," Champ volunteered. "And easier to work with than some of your babies. Take Penny, for example. Two years later she forgets which hand she's supposed to hurl the javelin with. Sometimes she even throws it onto the track. And Bucky still bucks plenty. Your high jumper Silk whines a lot. Kid Blast steps out of lane. The Lump's son dropped the shot on your foot. Hoo, sometimes—once in a while—even I tip a hurdle and fall down."

Sudden couldn't believe her ears: Mouth Champion admits a mistake!

She joined with Coach in a full, wholehearted laugh while Champ turned red, redder up around the neck of his UU Indians T-shirt. Redder than she'd ever seen. She tried to soothe him with, "I drop batons," but laughed more, for the first time, about her Vienna disaster.

Then they all laughed. At each other, at themselves. They laughed until they cried.

Brushing tears, finding his pen, wiping tears, filling his pen, blowing his nose, beginning to write—Coach said, "And I blow up in rage, Sudden. Terrible habit I must get over. I—I'll help you this minute. I'll write to the committee in longhand, submitting her world record. I'll swear to 3:59.9. I'll enter her name for the trials: Fox Running."

15

Bang.
Bang.
Bang.
Bang.
For all of those helping Fox train that May for the Olympic trials at the end of June, workouts began, middled, ended with a bang. Coach Calvin fired his starter's pistol each morning in the Cosmodome to get his runner accustomed to the sound and its echo. Muscular Rip took noon aim at the sky above the County Fair Grounds. Every weekend little Rosie blew holes in the sky over Moondance Resort, where they ran to expand their lungs in high altitude. Champ banged away indoors and out, polluting Uinta Valley with .32 caliber rings. His Bucky shot only from the mouth, bullet words about Champ's new Mescalero gun moll. Bucky was jealous, but Champ kept reloading the blanks.

Mark. Set. Bang.

Also Champ ran with Fox. Ahead, behind, next to her on Tartan turf for a week, then along her mossy trail when Fox suggested she might find a new herb for his health diet. "In the woods, one hour's run from here," she'd promised.

Champ elbowed her most of the way there. He blocked her view with his puffed-out sideburns. He tramped on her heels, spiked a bare toe for good measure. He shoved her into a foxhole. He tripped her from the side. He put the moves on her: stepped right if she tried to pass him outside; left when she came along their imaginary curb. He wouldn't let her pass him. He was pretending to be Bad Robin Minty, preparing Fox for her rugged trials. Champ ran Fox off the path into honeysuckle.

Fox never raised her fist or eyes. She ran unruffled in his dust. Once she said, "Old Leggings took me out to fight trees. He taught me to uproot them. Mescalero ritual." When Champ lagged to catch her words about her childhood, she sandwiched him between poplars and flew past him.

"Fox, good for you. Good lick!" Champ called, awed. "I wish I had your grandfather. He toughened you. What else did he teach you about competing?"

"Not competing. Surviving!" Sudden answered. She had joined them after her final exams. She'd managed to complete her courses while friends trained the Fox.

Champ hopped over a log. He squished mud. He whisked through ferns and spears of new grass. He hurdled small bushes. "Hurdling feels good outdoors. This is fun," he called to the front-runners. "Wait up."

Fox waited, up ahead among creepers.

"Hoo. Don't wait. Never take advice from runners in your race. They will try to trick you. They'll try to make you mad—psych you out. Don't pay attention to their help. Don't listen to their taunts, especially what they say at the starting line." Champ caught up with Fox. "Listen —practice on these, Fox. Practice ignoring."

Fox ran ahead.

Champ psyched her devilishly. "Wait up . . . your leg's got a gash . . . hey, stop a minute, you seem tired . . . hey, why not rest on the back-stretch . . . I'll rest with you."

Fox hung cool. She seemed to shut out his voice. She ran to her own music. Only twice did she break stride and call his name.

"Champ, be careful of that porcupine in the curve."

He answered from his leap. "Never, never warn a front-runner. Let her crash down and be darned. Just try to avoid the body. Up and over it like a hurdle." He jumped the sharp quills and kept on.

Fox warned him again. "Don't be afraid, Champ. A fox is passing you now."

Champion whirled in time to see an actual red fox bounding out of the meadow. He watched it cross his path and disappear into heavy foliage. He stopped to search for the sleek sight again. "Beautiful," he exclaimed. "Did you check that shade of red? That thick fur? That sort-of-smile on the snout? I've never seen a real fox before."

"Hardly any of them in the Cosmodome," Sudden said.

"It doesn't hurt to run outdoors now and then. You never know what you might see. Or eat. Try this." She handed Champ a shiny leaf. He chewed it up without a word except, "Nummmmm."

Fox whispered, "You will have good luck in your trials Brother. And you, Hart." She chanted a song of friendship with the fox. She spoke its language.

Bang.
Bang.
"Bangs won't bite. These blank bullets never kill. You're doing much better. But don't stand still to listen for the echo. Don't be skittish, Fox. Go."

All May, Fox ran efforts for Calvin in his Cosmodome. Quarter miles at nearly full speed. Rest, then 220s at top speed. Rest. Ten laps at half-speed, rest, a slow lap, rest, again the 220s, rest, again, rest, again. And always she ran with another runner on her heels or by her side, or slightly ahead, or way beyond—around a farther curve, yet in sight.

She kept them all within striking distance. She learned how far she might straggle behind the front-runner and still catch up at the finish. She learned to pass Rosie by making a quick, decisive move to the outside. No fooling around. Blow by. But not too wide. No wasted steps. Each footfall takes time, and time is precious.

She learned to pass Sudden on the bend when Sudden ran wide, into lane two. Fox slipped inside, sneaked along the curb in feather strides. She learned to pass Champion when he returned from his woods, where he ran every day now. Guld-sized Champ didn't yield when Fox swung right and around. He swerved into her path. Fox was forced to slow down. So she waited until he tired. One lap, two laps, three, and by him. Bye-bye, Champ-Guld. "I will see you at the tape," Fox said over her shoulder. Champ grinned at her hair.

June 1, Rip decided to rejoin the UU team for summer session. He ran back to the Cosmodome to be passed by the Fox. She learned to set her own pace, to break out in front of him at the bang, and to take each lap at an even speed. If Rip came abreast, she kept her same pace, whatever he said. Shoulders overlapping, they circled in step to her tune, not his words. If he passed her, she held firm, not tempted to run harder. She held firm if he fell behind, not tempted to widen the gap. She ran a fast, even pace: Her pace.

On. Fox practiced running through a field of six, one late afternoon mid-June.

Bang.

Fox shied, then left Bucky sulking at the start; passed Rosie inside at the first turn; circled with the pack, their fists whistling in her ears; caught Kid Blast on the far straghtaway and dueled him to the curve before going wide and by; he blasted almost even, but she blocked him in lane one, inched into two, and snuffed out his desperate challenge.

Ahead, clipping along in third place, Champ listened for her shoes. All quiet except Calvin on his platform, yelling through a megaphone. "Box Fox out. Box her out," he told his troops up the lanes. The echo of his voice covered Fox's tracks. She ran past Champ's muddy shorts, took third place by inches, inches, then feet. Yards ahead the Ripper showed his spikes. She let him lead her for a lap, for another, then increased her pace until she hung on his hoofs. "What is the matter?" she asked his hair ribbon.

He slowed, wondering. Am I bleeding or something? "Matter?" he asked. She ripped past his doubt. Into the home straight where Sudden, fresh in her mile, sprinted in first place. Above her Calvin yelled, "Kick now, Fox. Let's see your big kick. Do it! Do it!"

Fox did it. Fox kicking to the tape. Fox full of strength. Sudden full of strength, too. Her own. Fox and Sudden tying.

On. To Heaps of Pizza, where the seven athletes celebrated a 4:20 mile. Calvin said, "Mighty fine, considering Fox's hesitant start and that crunch at the first turn." Calvin ate pizza, which Fox passed among her friends. He said, "Excellent sauce. It tastes like sagebrush smells."

Champ told her with his mouth full, "Tastes like mountain laurel. My favorite leaf. The race is not only to the swiftest but also to the smartest. Hoo, you put a mental move on Ripper today. You foxed him out."

"For sure," Rip said. He laughed into his green peppers. His pigtail shook. "When Fox asked, 'What is the matter?' I thought my shorts might be falling off. Or my leg bleeding from her spike kick at the start. I slowed down to look at myself."

Fox narrowed her dark eyes in thought. "I am sorry I nicked you. I do not start well yet. The shoes are still strangers to my feet. The grass is not friends with my eyes." She paused. She put down her tray. With elbows out she pulled her curved index fingers toward her chest, like a bull pulling in its horns—Apache sign for "afraid." She said, "The gun is still hate in my ears."

"Why?" asked Coach and Rip and Champ and Rosie together.

But Fox went away with her tray full of dishes.

Bang. Bangbangbangbangbang.

For Sudden, Fox took starts until her ears cried out for relief. Bang, she gritted her teeth and stood still. Bang, she winced. Bang, she clenched a fist. Bang, she shook her head.

"Why?" asked Sudden. "Tell me so I can help you."

"That is all right. Shoot again. *Po'ednas.*"

All week the slow starts continued until bangbangbangbang Fox held her ears and knelt in a shower of leaves. "Live bullets," she whispered from the starting line that Sudden had drawn under an apple tree, their shelter from the late June sun.

"Right. Those were real bullets for the first time," said Sudden. "Are you more frightened? Or less? Can you tell the difference by their sound? Or only because leaves fell? Is it only the noise and smell that frighten you? Or the idea of bullets racing to a target? What ideas run through your mind? Ideas of a hit—a wound? Idea—" Sudden's voice trailed off into the sultry June air. She dropped the pistol and squatted under the shot-up apple tree. "Or have you a memory? Memory of a hit, a bullet wound? A death? What do you remember when the starter's gun goes off? What do you imagine can happen again?"

Fox shuddered.

"Something, Fox. The past? The night we found you?"

Sudden's eyes were drawn to Fox's. This brave girl had run on year-old legs down Dog Canyon; had run naked as a child to wasps and black widow sand tarantulas; had run at trees, trying to knock them over; had run away from school a dozen times to join her grandfather so they could scratch a living together; had run barefoot along New Mexico highways; had run Calvin's sprints and intervals, his punishing efforts; had run against the pain barrier of a sub-four-minute mile. What more painful memory? What vision more punishing? What terrible conclusion did Fox draw from the bang, smoke, and smell of burning powder?

Sun beat down through the skylight that real bullets had blown in their shelter. Sudden knew it was time to answer these questions before Fox went south to the trials next week, before she had to get off the line with world-class runners. Sudden shut her eyes and said, *"Talkona,"* to herself. Set. Go.

"Fox, it seems like the two of us should share our troubles." She pointed the empty pistol at a ladder. She squeezed the trigger. Click. Click. "Every race begins with this gun and ends with the string. I was afraid of the string." She massaged her throat where the finish line in Vienna had left its mark. "But Fox—not really the string. I know that now. More like the whole idea of racing. Of failing to win. Of losing the hundred meters or the relay. Of losing the fans, my coach, the reporters, other runners. I was afraid—"

"Not to be afraid," Fox broke into Sudden's confession.

"Afraid I'd lose my friends." Sudden gave Fox a long, absorbing look. And Fox seemed to understand. She whispered, "Old Leggings was afraid of the gun. I loaded it. I gave it to him." Then Fox sobbed. Tears seeped under her fists. Sweat flowed down her neck. "Old Leggings shot himself. Because he could not move. His legs —his hips were crushed. Old Leggings—under a horse." She broke down weeping. She didn't try to talk more.

Sudden knew what Fox was doing right then: retreating into her past, reliving the day of that bullet. Sudden wept with her. She saw Old Leggings lifting Fox Running to the moon, saw him sewing moccasins, painting suns and swifts and foxtails on their lodge, saw him printing Mescalero words in sand and mud and snow, teaching Fox to read a trail in her own language. Sudden heard the bang. *She* smelled the smoke. *She* saw Old Leggings falling backwards from the shot and dropping the gun. Sudden began to chant, "Not to worry," but quit right after "Not." She worried.

Until Fox chanted, too, her voice low and sad as the mourning dove. "Old Leggings wanted to die. He could never run again. He said, *'Mba'yen hutas,* you and I have strong legs. Our legs are our friends. When they die, we die. We will meet this bravely. It does not matter.' " Fox stood up. She walked toward the beehives. "He told me to load. He opened his mouth for the gun. He drank from it." Distance swallowed her tears and chant. Sudden followed to hear Fox say, I carried him into our *wickiup*. I covered him with his robe. I gathered kindling, struck flint. I made fire. I was not afraid. I wanted to die also." She spoke in Sudden's ear. "But when I ran away. I felt I killed him. I felt—I felt you catch me at the ravine. Then I knew I could hide at your school if I ran for your team. From Old Leggings to another, I went for help."

They had passed the beehives and entered a cornfield. Fox picked two young sprouts, gave one to Sudden. "Hand."

They both wiped their eyes on these green handkerchiefs. They blew their noses. They dug their feet into the fertile land and felt it gummy between their toes. They felt better. Restored. Cured by their words together. Fox said, "I will not shake at the starting gun, Hart. Will you run in the trials? Run the relay? For us? For yourself?"

Sudden promised, "Yes." She stuck the gun in her pocket and took off. Fox matched her foot for foot. They loped up rows of corn, disappearing into summer, running for the trials.

16

And at the Olympic trials everyone asked, "Who's the Indian girl?"

"The one with fierce eyes."

"That one with all the hair."

"The one over there drinking Dad's root beer with Kathy Hart."

"The only Indian around, meatheads. The only girl one

I've ever seen on a track," Robin Minty said to the seven girls warming up for Heat Two. Minty unzipped her shoe bag, took out her spikes, and began to sharpen them for *her* race. She sang, "My kind of race." She pulled off her sweat pants and taped on her wristbands. *"My* kind of race." She eased her University of Arizona sweat shirt over her pilot's glasses. "Absolutely my kind of race right here at *my* own home stadium."

Cheryl Gibbons said, "I think I met her before. Throws the javelin or shot."

"Who?" Minty had already forgotten Fox.

Gibbons nodded toward the tall calm girl up the track and whispered, "I saw her at the Garden around two years ago."

"Garden? Maybe the Indian Reservation Cactus Garden in Big Hip, Montana? Not *my* Madison Square Garden. I'd remember. I've run there the past three years. And the Colosseum. And the Astrodome. Every major mile. Once and for all, she's nobody." Minty squinted against the June Tucson sun. "Nothing but hot here."

Her words were lost in wind that blasted through the open north end of UA Stadium. The Arizona state flag snapped on its pole. Dust devils swirled through bleachers. At midfield the high-jump bar sagged, trembled, blew off its standard twice while Silk took her turns. Nearby the wind gauge spun up a storm. The gauge clerk held his hat crying, "No national records today, folksies. No state records. No stadium records will be set. Not in this gale."

Gibbons hollered over the wind and crowd. "Looks like that Indian girl's a runner or something. Seems to be hanging around for this heat. She's almost as big as Guld."

"Who?" Minty called, her back to the others. She was limbering, shaking her hands, jogging ten yards, tagging her feet. "Oh, the Indian." She turned to watch Fox, who remained at the starting line with Sudden. "What's her number? Anyone make out her number? What's her track suit say?"

"Can't see. It's a three. Or five. Or seven. Or—"

"Or any number in between," said Minty. "Cheryl, dope, you're a big help." She sat down again to tighten her spikes. "What gets me is why Kathy Hart's suited up. She hasn't raced in years. Not since she blew the relay in

Vienna. Anyone know if she's making a comeback or something?"

"It's four! Number four on the Indian's shirt. With a line in front of it like a bar or dash or hyphen. Or maybe a minus. Like that. Minus four." Gibbons stood on tiptoes trying to see over the man raking the long-jump pit. "And letters on the back of her shirt. F—O—X. Weird yellow shade to her shirt."

"Sort of goldenrod yellow," someone jabbered.

"Buttercuppy," said a girl in purple shorts.

"Dumb," Minty said to all of them and lay back in the worn, infield grass, awaiting the starter's call. "Fox Track Club must be. Is there such? No such—Fox University." She covered her eyes with a towel from her bag. She crossed her arms on her chest. Tight.

"She might be an actual Fox Indian. There *is* still a tribe. A girl Jim Thorpe. Thorpe was a Fox." One of the purple girls spoke. Gibbons wanted to know, "Who's Thorpe?" and the runners let her have it.

"Fox Indian, what I said."

"Bright Path was his real Indian name. I saw it on TV."

"From Oklahoma."

"That dude could do anything. Football, baseball. I saw the movie."

"Olympics—1912."

"Sweden. He won two gold medals."

Minty said, "Thorpe captured the pentathlon and decathlon. Fifteen events in all. Greatest athlete put-down of this century, that is until I run the first women's sub-four mile."

Minty sat up abruptly. "Say, I wonder if she really is a Fox Indian." Minty cleared her throat. "I wonder if she's related to Thorpe!" She cleared more. "Say, I wonder if she's running! In *my* heat. Oh-oh."

Wheet. The starter's whistle blew her from wondering. Resting bodies beside her sprang up and at 'em. Minty didn't. She studied her shoelaces, fidgeted with her socks, fussed around in her bag until she found a wad of gauze. She wiped off her glasses and forehead. She rose slowly, sauntered way behind the parade to the track, casually took her place in lane one. She untucked her shirt. She flexed her back muscles, causing her right elbow to dig Cheryl in lane two. "Previews of coming events," she said, glancing at Fox.

106

Gibbons muttered, "'When did you start using your elbows?"

If Fox saw or heard, she never let on. Her usual absorbed self, she waited in lane nine, Sudden by her side until the announcer told the crowd, "Heat number two of the mile. In lane one, Robin Minty of the University of Arizona." Mixed boos and cheers met her name. Minty only smiled. "Representing Florida State, in lane two, Cheryl Gibbons." Scattered clapping. From up high, a kid's voice piped out, "Don't forget, four laps make a mile. Cheree."

Sudden whispered, "Magic," to Fox, and shimmied toward her box seat through a clump of photographers. Several of them pestered her with questions: "Hey, Sudden, making a comeback? Where's your baton? Who's your dark-horse friend?"

"Ladies, to your marks," the starter called when the announcer had finished his list of girls in heat two. Nine runners spread out along the starting line. Each shook hands with the girl on either side, each except Minty. She kept her hands thrust in her armpits, as if warming them on this scorching day. Her shirt flapped in the wind. She ranted gloomily, "I'm very flat, just not up to this mile race. My legs feel mushy, like Cream of Wheat."

Gibbons, on her mark, whispered, "You always say that, Robin. You always complain. At the Astrodome last year you said you had terminal chicken pox. Then you won. It's getting so I won't believe you."

"Set."

Nine runners set.

Bang.

Bang.

"False start, lane two. You're rolling, Miss Gibbons."

Nine runners relaxed behind the line again. One jiggled in place; one stooped to jerk at the tongues of her Nike shoes; one waved to the press table; one unstuck a strip of leg tape and threw it to the curb; one filled her lungs with tense air; one dabbed a little spit on an old cinder burn. One stood very still. One growled, "Cher-yl, your false starts ruin my timing!" Gibbons asked, "Which lane was I in? I forget."

"Set."

Nine runners mustered.

Bang.

Bang.

"False start, lane nine. You must hold in there. Number four, er, Minus four. Don't try to beat the gun, all you ladies." He raised his arm, pointed the muzzle skyward.

"Set."

Bang.

The .32 flashed fire. A string of bodies broke smoothly forward, everyone except Fox, who held her mark a second extra. But she hadn't come unglued, hadn't wasted time holding her ears or shaking her head. She was starting now behind the wall of girls that gradually, gradually strung out in lane one. Gibbons led round the first turn, setting a fast pace for Minty, who ran on Gibbons' shoulder to hustle her along to even-greater speed. Two girls in purple hovered a step or so behind Minty; and the rest—stride by stride by stride—fell off the pace down the far straight. Back of them all at the second turn, Fox Running.

Fox running with her eyes on the leader, whose jumpy, uneconomical style was hypnotic: around and around, Gibbons' head. Up and down, tiptoe to heel, her feet. Right and left, her hands in broad swings. Gibbons, the wind-milling front-runner about to wind down some, be passed by a purple-shirted girl who was dodging Gibbons' flying fingers and dashing down the homestretch at

"64 seconds," called the chief timer. And "65, 67, 68" as one by one or two by two the others ran by.

"69.072," Calvin said to Sudden when their fox passed the timer, dead last.

But alive in every cell, Fox began to steer herself through the pack. Around the near turn a second time, she edged in front of a Long Beach Comet and a puffing Brooklyn Atom. On the backstretch she caught up with an anonymous striped shirt, went outside her, and into sixth place. Several strides ahead windmilled Gibbons, a tiring fourth-placer now. Between them, in fifth, a freckled girl hissed, "You're botching two lanes, Cheryl. Move it." Gibbons moved it: hips back and forth, arms over and under, shoes in and out of lane two. Freckles scampered up beside Gibbons in lane two-and-a-half. She cocked an elbow. Zap in ribs. Zip in front. Freckles ran free of Windmill Gibbons.

Fox Running took a different tack. She simply ran wide,

108

almost into lane three. Safely past Gibbons, she set her sights on the freckled shoulders rounding the curve. How to get by them without a puncture? Or fracture? Simple enough! Stay in lane three and go faster. Hold form and faster. Smooth. Faster. Faster into fourth place, she drove along the homestraight, came up on purple shorts at

"2:12," the chief timer blared over the crowd, which had livened up with this third lap. Fans called to their favorite runners.

"Pour it on, Gibbons."

"Minty hold 'em off, you cutthroat."

"Way to run, Injun."

"Mba'yen hutas," Calvin yelled in the tumult, speaking Fox's language now, her name in Apache.

The fox may have heard. With shocking power she pulled even with purple shorts, flashed by them, around the curve, cut into lane one, and tried to hug the straight-away curb, inside second-place Minty. Fox shortened her stride, took careful, delicate steps in an effort to wiggle her way. Minty snarled like a timber wolf, "Off my back, Minus four." If Fox heard, she didn't yield. She started to run through the small opening, but Minty boxed her out. Fox changed stride, pulled back, drifted into lane two, spurted, ran neck and neck with the killer. Then, in a flurry of action, Minty shot out her right elbow, sharp as a scalpel. Again and again she lunged it at Fox, who ran wider and wider to avoid contact. Wider and suddenly past Minty—Fox untouched, not bothered, not surprised to be in second place, alone at

Bang.

Below them, Fox Running slowed. Sudden and Calvin hollered questions at each other over the groaning crowd. "Didn't you?" "No, didn't you?" "Why, oh why?"

"Keep running, Injun." A third voice farther down the track.

"Muhs'dasa." Calvin and Sudden, a duet to the frightened girl.

They'd forgotten to warn Fox about the gun lap! All that training. All their advice. Yet neither had explained to their bang-shy girl that the starter fires once again at the beginning of the last lap—the gun lap: a noisy signal in case the runners have lost track of distance in the heat of competition. A bang of encouragement. Last yards to run, last turns around the track.

Fox faltered, clenched her fists, ducked her head. The crowd screamed advice while Fox moved as if she were running up to her knees in water.

"Your form. Regain your form, Number four."

"Don't crash, girl."

"Do it, Minus Fox," piped the kid upstairs.

Fox didn't it. She didn't capsize. And she didn't give up when all the others swooped down on her and by. As at Iffley she took herself in tow. Her legs knew the way if her head didn't. She set out. Once more she pelted around the close turn. She drove herself relentlessly toward eight on the straightaway. One by one she passed each blur of arms and legs: Comet, Atom, Stripes, Gibbons, Freckles, Purple I, Purple II, until only Minty at the home turn rumbled between Fox Running and the unbroken tape.

Fox kicked her searing kick. Closer and closer she came to the cutthroat Minty. In seconds she was abreast. Again she drew a formal glare of hate from Minty.

And Minty's casual spike when Fox sprinted ahead! Minty's shoe raked Fox's leg, leaving an awful graze. Fox slowed again, this time in pain, only inches from the tape. In a wild, finishing thrust, Minty sprang home in first place. She ran directly into a victory lap, icily watching the wounded second-placer over her shoulder: Fox bleeding.

Then Fox hobbling off the track.

By the time Fox got back to the locker room her shoe had filled with blood. Leaning on Sudden, she sloshed a red-splattered trail to the trainer's table. She lifted herself up for examination. Sudden said, "Everywhere Minty races there's carnage. She's a mean thumper."

Fox answered, "Accident. It does not matter." She winced when Sudden touched the gash and called for the UA team doctor. While they waited, Sudden unlaced the gummy shoe, flung it away for good, then washed Fox's foot and leg with alcohol.

"Seven stitches worth," the doctor announced. She set to work on Fox without another word except to apologize for the long needle of Novocain. When Calvin showed up, he did all the talking.

"Fox, you went too wide when passing, but otherwise you ran beautifully. Robin Minty should be disqualified. I just spent twenty minutes trying to convince the judges."

Fox said, "It was an accident. Not to disqualify." She bit her tongue and stood down on her leg. She limped to the shower.

Calvin called after her. "Second place puts you into the finals tomorrow. Come on out and watch Guld run her heat." Louder. "You can size her up."

"Your girl cannot race tomorrow," the doctor said emphatically. She packed her needles and thread. "Fox cannot." She and her medicine bag set off in search of another Minty victim, leaving Calvin and Sudden dumb with disbelief.

Mournfully they eyed each other across the examining table. Calvin seemed near crying. Sudden, embarrassed, paced away with lowered head, kneeing locker doors shut. "Take it easy, Sudden," Coach choked out. "Your final heat is coming up. Don't mess around with your knees."

"I don't care anything about my stupid legs," Sudden barked.

"I do—and about Fox's leg. If she can't run tomorrow, well, she can't. Resign yourself and wait'll next year for the national championships. Four years for the next Olympic trials. I'll wait. I must. I learned my lesson when I insisted you race with a torn muscle. You'd of never dropped the baton if you hadn't been in pain. Your drop was my fault—my—"

His cracking voice trailed off into the background of water falling. Steam seeped out of the shower room. They listened to distant splashings, gigantic tears like those they both fought back. Splat. Raining down on their injured runner. They heard Fox chanting under water: "Wind blowing. Rain starting. Miles waiting. I will feed my leg."

Sudden's head jerked up. Her eyes gleamed. She sniffed the air, smelled nothing but Lifebuoy and athlete's-foot powder. She rushed to the window, threw it open, felt the freshening wind. She drew a gulp. She said, "Coach, it's gonna rain. Soon. Tonight? No, tomorrow. Nyégò! These trials will be postponed a day. Two, maybe."

Calvin strode to the locker-room door, out and back. "There's half a sun, a stiff wind, a few grayish clouds. The same as yesterday, the day before. What do you know about rain?"

111

"Fox knows weather. She has powers from Old Leggings. She taught me. Believe us three, it will rain."

"Right," chanted Fox, between them in a bathrobe that was way too short for her. Her leg looked better already. She wasn't limping. Coach brightened. He joined the chant. "I'd better hike to the hotel for my umbrella." He left to catch Guld's heat.

Fox missed Guld's win. She stayed in the locker room reading the *Official Olympic Rules Book*. She took her time dressing but was at the line for Sudden's comeback race. Fox watched the dash girls loosening thumb screws on their blocks, moving toeholds forward or backward. Sudden settled into hers, tested them, pressed her toes against the rubber pads, sprang out a few steps, then back to wait for, "On your mark." Sudden wasn't worried. She felt strong. She knew that four girls would be chosen from today's heats for the Olympic relay team.

"Mark."

Plus two alternates would be chosen in case a team member got sick or injured.

"Set."

Six altogether. She knew she'd be one of those six.

Bang.

And in 10.5 seconds she was. She would be running anchor leg in the Olympics. Fastest girl, carrying the baton into the tape at Los Angeles. Another chance to drop—or not to drop. A chance to show Coach. No, to show Fox—no, to show herself.

Coach chortled. "You came off the blocks exactly like you used to. Suddenly. You ran your usual race—out front the entire distance. Some old lady you are! But I notice a new facial expression."

"She did not grind her teeth at the start," said Fox.

"For fifty meters her lips turned up. Around eighty I saw her eyes crinkle."

"That's called a smile, Coach." Sudden smiled another one and wiped her forehead. From habit, not from sweat.

Going for the hotel, Coach and his runners picked their way across an infield full of girls at rest or ready among their shoes bags, sweat suits, discuses, shots, javelins. Fox nearly stumbled on a javelin and remarked that it would fly farther with eagle feathers attached to the shaft. Coach agreed and pointed to the tip. "That could be deadly on a hunting trip for moccasin leather."

Sudden shushed them both. She nodded to Minty in the grass, towel over her head and yelling, "Hey, trainer-man, where's me some tape for this scratch?"

The three slipped by her unnoticed, for Coach held his temper. He said, "I'll tape your leg tomorrow, Fox. If it rains—I mean *while* it rains you'll stay off it completely." He guided them home for the night.

Stay off it Fox did, through a hot, rainless night, a day of thundershowers, a clearing night, a day of intermittent cloudbursts too frequent for final races. Fox read the rules book. And reread it. Sudden tried to concentrate on the *Mescalero Poem Book* to keep her mind off stitches and gunshots. Coach prowled the stadium barefoot, reporting a flash flood on the homestretch and a slushy javelin run-way. He was delighted by these. Rain gave them time. Fox could heal. When at last the track and field dried out, Fox seemed ready to run.

So did Minty, Guld, Purple II, and five others who had qualified for the finals. "The first three finishers will represent the United States of America at the Olympics in Los Angeles, two months from today," an official voice trumpeted as the milers lined up. Fox wore a bandage of surgical tape, same color as her Sub-4 shirt. Minty wore dark glasses. Her shirt was freshly stitched with GONE where UA had been on the back. More aloof than ever, Guld lounged tall in lane one, her gold uniform fresh as Champ's used to be.

Sudden studied the starters. What were their plans for each lap? Guld's tight expression kept her secrets. Mean Minty's covered eyes gave no clues, but her mouth be-trayed her. She yelled, "I'm so sleepy . . . sacroiliac aches . . . discus-size goose bumps . . . or mumps on my knees. . . . Hey, Sub-four, I notice your leg's in a sling. No miracle miles for you today, eh?" Yes, Robin Minty's psych-out tactics. Complain and needle. Com-plain and needle Fox. Psych Fox out, then toss an elbow and fist and spike.

And then what?

Deep in thought, Sudden missed the "mark," "set," and "bang."' All at once she saw Fox at the starting line, Fox standing alone.

But hurrah! Fox not tumbling, not even trembling. Fox

113

only confused by Minty's parting shot, Minty's hand formed into a gun, her forefinger poking Fox's ribs, her loud mouth saying, "BOOM BOOM. Gotcha twice, scaredy-fox." Minty must have spent her rainy days in research about Fox's fear, asking reporters questions, checking with the entry judges.

At the starting line, Fox's eyes uncrinkled. Her lips turned from up to straight across. She added her stony fighting face to her uniform. She bucked off the line a little behind the ganged-up others. Guld set a scorching pace, Minty clung to her shoulder, and everyone else tried to stay with the leaders.

Not Fox. She ran two laps as if her stitches itched or leg smarted—a slow, jarring, broken rhythm that kept her in last place. Going into the near curve for the third time, Fox raised her hand to her mouth. To stifle a cry? To bite her knuckles in pain?

When that hand came down it spanked her flanks. She picked up speed. Her body came to order. She fixed her narrowed eyes on the scramble. Sprinting and shoving, Minty took over first place from Guld. A boxed runner stumbled. A passing runner veered and tangled with Purple II. Both crashed to the straightaway. Runners slowed to hop bodies. Tiring runners slowed. The clump became a single file that Fox joined as a tail, a red one, her own black mane a last-place banner at the gun lap.

Bang.

Gun or Minty yelling, Fox didn't care. Only her ears shuddered. Her legs and arms sped on. On. On past. On through and among and around and between the others. In front of everyone but Guld a-huff in the final curve. And Minty. Fox whipped herself. She inched between the two leaders. She listened to Guld's shoes fade. TAP, TAp, Tap, tap. She glanced from side to side to see if anyone else was moving past fast. Side to side, glance ahead, side to—

Fox saw a gleam of metal, a javelin in air. This deadly mistake flew nearer! A javelin misthrown from the infield, where the thrower must have slipped as she ran down the still wet runway. The javelin's sharp point sailed toward the finish line. The tip glinted its warning to Fox. She broke stride, shouted to the girl ahead.

"Minty, stop! Robin. STOP. Dòdà. Dòdà."

114

Minty lifted her knees even higher. Faster. Her shirt said GONE and she was, in a kicking finale.

Then—then—then down in a heap, legs tangled with the javelin's aluminum shaft: Mighty Minty on her back, five yards this side of the finish string. Fox hurdled the jav and Minty's broken sunglasses and won the race.

Fox paused for breath. She leaned on the finish post, her weight off her sore leg. She ignored the crowd's call for a victory lap and trotted back to pull the weeping Minty to her feet. Minty wailed, "I thought you were trying to psyche me out when I heard 'STOP.' Or put some Apache curse on me."

Bang.

The starter fired his gun once again, a salute to Fox, to her victory over pain, to her good sportsmanship. Fox barely heard the shot or the cheers. Her ears were covered first by Guld's long arms in a hug, then by the third-place girl's upstretched hands. Fox hugged them back.

These three would run against each other and against the world in the Olympics. Not Fox's familiar mile, either. Instead, the 1500-meter distance, slightly less than a mile. For Fox that meant new tactics to plan. More training all summer. Miles and meters to go. Scenery and Sudden ahead. Fresh fields to conquer, green fields to roam with her friend until August 30.

"No give-up in you Mescaleros," shouted a reporter who followed the winner to her locker. Holding a camera high over Coach and the doctor and Sudden, a photographer shot Fox—hair, eyes, teeth, —4, open hands, stitches, bare feet. Flashbulbs pop pop pop pop. Fox Running for the world to see.

17

No one asks anymore, "Who's the redskin . . . squaw . . . Indian . . . Apache girl . . . runner . . . winner . . . Fox Running?"

They all know.

She's the one who warned Bad Minty of the off-target javelin at the Olympic trials, the one who whipped Big Guld and Windmill Gibbons and every other ranking miler in the U.S.A. Fantastic! The one supposed to have run a world-record mile on a high-school track in northern Utah. A secret race with the clock, her time something like 3:59.9. Impossible! Not for her. A Mescalero, can you beat that? New Mexico tribe, in case you hadn't heard. All her tribesmen thought she was dead, burned up with her grandfather in a fire. They found a pile of bones and never looked further.

But is *she* ever alive! She's a student at Uinta University summer school. On athletic scholarship, naturally. Trains with Champion Davis, Kid Blast Huish, Jack Flake, little Rosie Graham, and others up there in the mountains; the Heaps of Pizza gang they call themselves. Kids coached by Guy Calvin. Calvin even runs with them. Outside, for miles, they say. In all kinds of weather. Runners hardly ever use that fancy factory of his anymore—the Cosmodome—except for track meets.

Calvin has the magic touch this summer. No one quits on him. And the best part is that he and Fox Running brought the old lady back for another try at the relay. Terrific! Sudden Hart will be running anchor leg. Her pal Fox is running third leg of the very same race. One of the regulars tore a ligament, another wants to concentrate on her own hundred-meter dash. An alternate got married and quit. So Fox volunteered for the race. Naturally! Maybe just to team up with Sudden, who can say? That Fox is still pretty mysterious. But oh so fast. Fast enough to run first leg, but everyone knows she's still a little bit gun-shy. Besides, she wants to hand the baton to Hart in the passing zone tomorrow.

"Hand," says Fox.

Fox and Sudden run the Colosseum track together the night before their Olympic relay in Los Angeles. Fox touches box seats, flagpoles, starting posts, finish posts, as if to leave her scent for others to follow. She and Sudden practice exchanging the baton with a pen Fox always carries in her pocket: Champ's gift when she'd won her UU scholarship.

Fox says, "This pen is the same color as our stick tomorrow. Black as the raven."

Sudden takes the pen. "Funeral color. I hope not my funeral—my drop." Sudden can't help saying the hated word. They both slow to a walk.

"Hart, I carved our relay stick from black wood. Utah wood. A tree we both ran to in many leaves. Take the stick from me tomorrow. Hold it hard. Feel it. Feel it until you cross the finish line ahead of all others."

Back and forth her pen travels between the two friends. Surehanded Sudden palms it, pretending the pen's clip is an arrow. Surefooted Fox, steady in darkness, jogs them both to the third passing zone.

"You will stand here waiting for me. Look down! I will draw our magic signs right where you place your shoes tomorrow." With the pen she makes

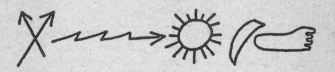

Then Fox jumps up and catches her friend's hand, presses the pen there. Sudden's hand is open, warm, eager for the stick. Fox says, "Hand. Now you draw us a sign for good luck."

Sudden thinks for a long time, one of the many lessons she's learned from her fox. She thinks until Champion calls, "Hoo, wait up and we'll go home together," from the hurdles he's been testing a final time before his own race tomorrow. She thinks he's been testing a final time before his own race tomorrow. She thinks until Coach Calvin comes to escort his three stars to the Olympic Village dorms.

Finally Sudden kneels and draws Gigantic. It almost overflows into the next lane, where South Africa will be running the relay.

"All our hearts are bigger," Sudden explains to the three—and to herself. "When you exercise as much as we have, your heart grows huge. That's the logical result of our running. Exercise just any old muscle and it expands. You see, hearts are only muscles. Red and tough and slippery—"

"All the better to feel with," whoops Champ to the relayers. Coach crosses his arms over his chest, Apache sign language for love. "All the better for this," he says to his Olympians.

Hart squeezes the pen and races out of the passing zone. She calls, "I'll hold this baton forever if Fox will promise not *even* to flinch tomorrow at the"

18

Bang.

From her position at third leg, Fox heard the shot. A far-off thunk, really. More like the sound an arrow makes hitting a stump target, she thought. Fox glanced down to make sure her feet were placed just right in the passing zone. She looked around the bend at Hart waiting top of the homestretch. Fresh Hart, hoarding her energy, ready to blow it on the anchor leg. No sign of Hart's nerves. They smiled at each other across one hundred meters. Then Fox turned slightly to watch her lead-off runner in the star-spangled shirt—U.S.A. sprinting forth, behind Russia, Canada, and West Germany. Seconds later those stars flittered into the passing zone—U.S.A. dead last.

To Fox, at such a distance, the baton exchange seemed smooth enough. Up close it wasn't. Americans in the crowd let out a huge gasp when their second-legger bobbled the stick. Everyone else kept eyes on the first-place duel: Russia—Canada; no, Canada; no, Russia; no Canada; no, Russia; no, West Germany leading; West Germany surging ahead, her wild, excited face coming closer to Fox's still-smiling one. Fox didn't notice West Germany. Her eyes held only the U.S.A.'s baton that pumped toward her in a shaky fist. The fist approached her passing zone. Closer. Pumping closer. Pumping shakily closer. Fox turned around, away from the fist, and started to run, forming her own steady fingers and thumb into a "V." She listened for "Hand." She heard "Hand" and closed her "V" around the baton.

I will take this stick quickly to Hart, she thought.

This magic stick that Fox had wrestled from the lightning-struck tree in their home pasture! This blackened wood she had cut from the trunk scratched with 10.5. This 11-inch stick she had carved with Mescalero words and signs after reading the *Official Olympic Rules Book*:

119

"The baton is a tubelike object made of wood, metal, or paper, which is passed from one runner to another in a relay race. The length shall not be more than 11.8 inches or less than 11 inches; the circumference shall not be more than 4.7 inches or less than 4 inches; the weight shall not be more than 1.76 ounces." Fox had found no printed rules in the record book against lightning-struck wood, against carving the wood—against magic!

Not to worry, Hart. Not to drop this chunk of love.

With one stride Fox passed South Africa, Cuba, Great Britain, Australia. With two she wiped out Russia and Canada. Another and she grabbed the lead from West Germany, the lead and rousing "Bravos" from the crowd, more and more as she streaked toward Hart. A deafening noise after seventy meters. Not to deafen Hart, Fox thought, getting ready to shriek, "HAND!"

"*Axàhy*," Fox said in her natural low voice.

Instead she'd said an Apache *Hart* and handed her friend a ten-meter lead along with the baton. She felt Hart's gentle tug mid-stick, right where the carved crescent moon joined a rising sun. She felt Hart slide her fingers farther along the chain of baby feet and zigzags of lightning. Fox imagined Hart's face as she discovered their favorite words and realized what kind of baton she held. Hart's blue eyes alight, lips drawn back in her biggest grin—Hart Winning.

Then that stick was on its way to the finish line in the sure grip of a confident front-runner.

And here's what Fox saw as Hart covered those final 100 meters of the Olympic 4 x 100-meter relay. Fox saw Russia bolt into second place, West Germany drop to third. She saw Canada drop her baton and Cuba kick it across seven lanes. She saw West Germany drop to fourth, South Africa pull up lame and drop out of the race, and West Germany drop to fifth. She saw Australia drop back, drop back, drop back; Great Britain drop off, drop . . .

"Hart, not to drop" whispered Fox in the crowd's roar.

Hart held. Hart ahead in a potent sprint, faster, faster, faster, faster, just when she appeared to be going all out. Speed without strain. First place without sweat. Fun-running. A four-legged animal romping, or so it seemed to Fox, who watched Hart's starred shirt merge with fluffy, piled clouds in the distance. There, alert in the clouds, timekeepers hung ready to freeze Sudden's race into the *Olympic Record Book*. Photographers lurked beside the finish post, snapping that stampede, snapping the startling instant that Hart hit the thin white ribbon, dragging it forward with her a hundred feet. Then Hart slowed, tapered off, cooled down, listened to the crowd's clamor just as she used to.

No, not as she used to, for today she heard only gibberish. Not bravos, huzzas, not praise for Sudden. She heard waterfowl gabbling, bears gurring, tons of bees buzzing, and locusts churring. She heard the sounds of her mountain training.

"Whoooooooooooooo ha," Sudden finally sorted out of the wildlife chorus.

"Aw-right! You're aw-right!" But praise didn't matter.

"SSSSSSSSSSSSSSSSSSudden." Not even her own name in crescendo.

"Sudden. Sudden Unbutterfingers." She recognized Champ and Coach. They mattered.

"Magic stick. Magic Hart." Fox talking. Fox mattered more. Fox ran to hug the anchor leg. Hart threw her baton into the air for joy.

That stick cast its spell again. The losers calmed down. Enraged Canada gave up stomping on the sidelines. West Germany got it together with a cheer for the U.S.A. Crying Australia wiped her eyes on her shirt number and walked over to congratulate Hart, who pointed to Fox, who pointed to their other two team members. All four U.S.A. relayers clustered around the ceremonial platform. They mounted it on signal and bent their heads to receive gold medals on long, long ribbons. Way off in the background a crowd of geese, bears, bees, and locusts sang "The Star-Spangled Banner." Fox chanted along. She came out strong on, "Land of the free/And the home of the *brave*." In Hart's ear she added, "We Mescaleros always say, 'You have a good heart,' when we mean *brave*."

Coach Calvin called, "Fox, save your breath. You run again in exactly one hour." He stood below the winners, grinning up. He reached for Hart, lifted her down, and swung her to and fro. Her ribbon wound around both their necks. A gold medal smacked his Adam's apple. He said, "Fox's third leg was the finest curve running I've ever seen. She took it low, controlled, faster than—"

By then Hart's army swarmed their superstar, calling

and hallooing. "Great comeback, Kathy!" "Attagirl." "Waytogo, Legs!" "You sure can scoot, 10.5." "Whatja eat? Howdja train?"

Hart didn't answer.

"Sudden, you are something else!" One reporter summed it up. "You moved like a playful deer out there. How many of Calvin's efforts did you run every day to keep from losing the baton?"

"She never lost," Calvin said sharply. "Someone else just came in first four years ago." He dragged his two champions through the yipping reporters.

One of them shouted, "Your young Fox-cub is sensational, too, Guy. She's the next Kathy Hart."

Right up to that moment Hart had said nothing. But abruptly she hollered, "She's not the *next* anyone. She's Fox Running *now*. Catch her in the fifteen-hundred-meter final if you can." With a wave to her fan club she disappeared after the Fox.

For the next fifty minutes Calvin and Hart and Fox sat together in the coaches' section, rows of padded chairs behind a flag-draped barrier along the final curve. Hart worried about the starter's gun. She knew she shouldn't worry, knew Fox had probably—had almost—had maybe licked her fear of the big bang. So Hart pretended not to worry. She did this and that to put Fox at ease. She toweled off Fox's black braid, which wasn't even damp. She surrounded her with a warm-up jacket. She broke out a canteen of Wasatch Lake water and forced a sip on Fox, who coughed because she was lying down across five seats, soon coolly dozing while Coach lectured on tactics.

"Miss Guld's no slouch, we already know that. Try to dust her off early. She'll get discouraged. Then just sit in on the Chinese girl, Mei Zee, for the second lap. Let her pace you. Hang on to her heels. Watch your lap times on the clock if you can't hear them over the crowd. That Kenyan girl hasn't looked sharp in her qualifying meters this week, but you can bet she'll be the front-runner. Stay back and watch her. And listen. You'll hear when she tires out. Huffpuffing. You can probably launch your attack at the end of lap three. Don't get boxed. Don't bump anyone. Don't . . ."

Fox dozed on. She didn't hear Bucky's slurred whistle of greeting or Rosie's "Lotzaluck" when they came to

122

wish her well. But she felt a feather tickle her nose. She sneezed awake to find Rip's gift, a feather from the red-tailed hawk, hooked in her hair. In her hand, Champ's silver medal he'd won for the hurdles: second place. Champ said, "Hoo, Fox. Scratch my medal. It's the real silver stuff. But you're better. You're gold—and red."

Coach said quietly, "Oh, forget about all my fussy tactics, Fox. Go out there and just pass everyone in a different-colored shirt."

"No, just pass everyone a different color," Champ whooped, taking back his silver. "You're the one."

"Right," everyone said at the same time, everyone together but Fox, who moved toward the starting line with graceful strides. Once more she nodded greetings to the runners on each side of her. Once more she looked down to see her toe on Tartan turf, looked up to see a sky full of wispy clouds hiding the sun at intervals. Then her eyes straight forward, on the gun butt that lapped over the starter's back pocket.

"Ladies, take your marks," he said, drawing his pistol and in the same motion pointing it at the nearest cloud.

The crowd went deathly silent, cringing some of them, Sudden among them, expecting the bang within seconds.

"Set."

The crowd heard the gun, too. Right then: magnum force at the starting line, bringing the entire stadium instantly to its feet for this final getaway, a spreading boom echoing like the report of a cracked cannon. Yes, of course. Everyone heard the

19

Everyone but Fox. She heard instead a whisper from Old Leggings. "Run now, my little baby." She felt him lift her off the mark, felt the tough, weathered skin of his hand in hers when he urged her forward through a herd of racers. She cantered free, then saw him ahead at the first turn. He beckoned her with his elk-hoof rattle. He war-danced in place. She flew past him and Guld with the same step. Seconds later, on the back straightaway, she saw him again. He seemed to be leaning against the door of their *wickiup*. Juniper boughs framed his hearty smile. At the far turn he chanted, "This way, my strong one," and led her into a battle of elbows. For her he parried blows to the starting line. He waved a wreath of fresh willows and was gone.

So was Fox, into the second lap. She hadn't heard the lap time.

She heard instead familiar voices calling warnings and encouragement as she strode hair to hair with Mei Zee. From a box seat on the curve Rosie told her to, "Watchit, watchit, watchit!" Fox just saved herself in time from a Chinese jostle. From the grandstand Rip called, "Loose and cool. For sure, loose and cool!" Her own feet answered chuff, chuff, chuff, chuff on the furnace-hot track. To her that green Tartan felt like spruce needles. She scuffed tons of them out behind herself, into the slowing shoes of Zee. From their seats along the homestretch Bucky and Champ spoke Mescalero for the first time. They approved of Fox in unison: "Make 'em all look like cripples, *Mba'yen hutas*!" The rest of the crowd hushed, eyes on a gigantic clock that winked seconds beginning the third lap.

Fox didn't see those blue numbers.

Instead she saw Akii-Ouko, a Kenyan ten yards ahead. The black girl gave no sign of letting up her furious pace. Fox followed her spike sparks from turn to straight to turn, where Guy Calvin waited behind the low concrete barrier, shouting advice. Something about "shove." No, about "love." "Love!" His words were lost in the crowd's sudden rumble when Fox made her move around Akii. On. On. Red and black, shoulder to shoulder. Time for a hurried glance at Coach for his help. He tapped his heart, Apache sign language for *father*. With that, Fox became front-runner.

She missed the bang at the gun lap.

Fox heard instead the crowd drum their seat backs and scream, "World record, go for it." Their massed voices reached a peak when Fox snapped into her feathery kick. She shut out their din. She sprinted for sheer joy.

124

Her feet caressed the track. She journeyed from landmark to landmark alone in that huge stadium. She thought, There is my own curve, easy going like around our lake. I will trail a flock of quail here. And this backstretch feels fine to me, as friendly as my home mesa. Only here are no trees I must flatten. Just someone panting behind me. Old Leggings trying to catch up. I will beat him to camp for once.

Fox ran loose, deep into the final turn, like a sunbeam streaming before the delirious crowd.

Sun, full and yellow, filled half the sky. Doves of peace winged above the stadium. Balloons rose from the stands in four directions: Every-colored smoke signals. Coach smelled gold. Rosie and Rip, Champ and Bucky, saw red feet kissing the final fifty yards. Fox felt her own legs in a green meadow bounded by a wisp of string—string coming nearer.

Hart came nearer.

Instead of string, Hart was there. All at once she had Fox in her arms, holding her safe from timers, judges, announcers, reporters, racers, coaches—fans at the finish line. Neither of them heard the loudspeaker in six languages: "The youngest—the fastest—the first girl to—an American Indian in world-record time." Nor their national anthem as Fox climbed the narrow steps to the first-place platform.

And there was Fox turning to face eighty thousand clappers, Fox beaming, Fox raising high her hand holding the red feather, Fox leaning for her second gold medal, Fox reading upside down and aloud the medal's inscription, Fox calling, "Sudden," to her friend at crowd's edge, Fox loping a victory lap of that Olympic track, then Fox and Hart Running, Running Home.

R. R. KNUDSON was born in Washington, D.C., and grew up in Arlington, Virginia. She received a B.A. from Brigham Young University, and M.A. from the University of Georgia, and a Ph.D. from Stanford University. After fifteen years of teaching English, R. R. Knudson became a full-time writer. She lives in Sea Cliff, New York, in a house overlooking Long Island Sound.

In researching FOX RUNNING, R. R. Knudson spent an extended period of time on the Mescalero Apache Indian reservation in New Mexico. Running is one of her passions, and she trained with the University of Arizona track team in 1974 for a close-up look at the lives of racers. FOX RUNNING is her fourth novel for young readers.